The Tycoon's Baby Revelation

Revelation

The Abbot Sisters Series

Elizabeth Lennox

Table of Contents

Chapter 1

Sloane stepped out of the beat up Chevy hatchback, nervously tugging her skirt down over her hips and taking a deep breath. "This is it," she whispered, looking up at the non-descript building.

It wasn't much to look at. Just a two story structure surrounded by a bunch of other two story buildings. "Is this the right place?" she muttered through numb lips. Pulling up the e-mail on her phone, she checked the address, then looked at the building again. Yep. This was the right address.

She walked carefully in the borrowed black heels, hoping that she wouldn't fall on her face and land in a humiliating heap on the simmering hot asphalt. She'd never worn heels before. Sneakers had been the shoes of choice while working at the fast food restaurant where Sloane had been employed for the past four months.

Glancing down at her skirt, she smoothed out the wrinkles, hoping it didn't look too shabby. Sloane's youngest sister, Pepper, had miraculously presented this outfit to her this morning, her eyes shimmering with anxious pride. "I got the skirt and blouse out of the donation box at the shelter a few days ago," Pepper had explained with a hopeful expression in her eyes. Eyes that were too old and wary for a four-teen year old. "It's good material, although the style is dated." She'd smoothed her hand down over the tan material. "I was able to adjust the size so that the skirt would fit you better and so that it didn't look so...worn out."

Rayne, the middle sister of their trio, had handed her the black pumps. "Martha gave me these," she told Sloane. "She needs them back though. But we've all got our fingers crossed for your job interview today."

Sloane swallowed past the lump of emotion in her throat, so damned proud of her sisters she could barely stand it. Sure, the three of them were homeless at the moment, sleeping at a shelter each night and eating their meals in the buffet line that the church across the street cooked for the residents. But they'd all been working hard, saving every penny and finding odd jobs so that they'd have a few extra dollars. Between the three of them, they'd almost scraped up enough money to rent a studio apartment. They wouldn't have furniture, not for a while, but it would be really great to not have to sleep with one eye open every night, fearful of the other shelter guests stealing their stuff or...or worse.

Standing here now, in the altered suit and borrowed shoes, Sloane lifted her chin with determination. "I can do this!" she whispered fervently. "I can!"

Applying for this administrative assistant's position had been a long shot, but Sloane had decided that she had nothing to lose by trying. Working at a fast food place just wasn't bringing in enough money to protect her sisters and things were scary at the homeless shelter. The three of them stuck together for security, but...it was still dangerous.

Taking a deep breath, Sloane pulled open the door and, with as much feigned confidence as she could muster, stepped into the blank-looking building and...froze.

There wasn't much in the building. No offices, no walls, no desks, or... well, nothing. It was literally a shell of a building, with even the overhead wires hanging down in some places.

But there were about ten or twelve stunningly beautiful women sitting in what looked like a space that might eventually become a lobby – but at the moment, was just a concrete floor, ceilings that revealed the electric wires and ventilation system and no walls.

The gorgeous women didn't seem to mind the lack of an office environment, Sloane realized. In fact, most of them were too busy preening, flipping their glossy blonde or brunette hair back over their shoulders or fluffing their locks for additional volume. One woman held up a mirror, pursing her lips and batting her lashes as if practicing for some sort of audition.

This was odd, Sloane thought nervously as she took the only empty seat in the room. There were so many other women, all sitting on uncomfortable, metal folding chairs, all of them waiting impatiently to be called, all shooting covert glances at the others, as if measuring up their competition. When their names were called, they jumped up, excited and eager for their interview.

Sloane didn't understand what was going on until one of the women, a blonde woman with red, glossy lips and a cream silk blouse that was so low cut, Sloane could see the edge of her black, lace bra, sneered in her direction. "Why don't you just walk away now? *I'm* going to land this job and," she smiled maliciously, "if I'm lucky, land Josh Starke as well."

One of the other women, a blonde with shimmering hair and red lips, sneered at both of them. "Give it up, beeatch," she whispered with a vicious, condescending laugh. "You don't have what it takes to win Josh Starke's attention," and she lifted her hands to cup her very bodacious breasts slightly.

Two other women sitting nearby snorted and Sloane watched with crazy fascination as yet another woman unbuttoned one more button on her silk shirt.

Perhaps she should walk away, Sloane thought. The other women were all stunningly beautiful and all had amazing figures. After six months of near starvation, of giving nearly all of the food that she could afford to her younger sisters so that they could concentrate at school, Sloan looked like the homeless person that she was. Pepper might have done a good job of altering the skirt and blouse, but none of her sister's efforts could compare to the gorgeous, expensive outfits these ladies were wearing.

Which begged the question...what was going on here? Who was Josh Starke and why were all of these women preening as if they were about to step onto a stage for a beauty contest?

Furthermore, the building was empty, without office furniture, lighting, phones, computers...or even walls! So...was this even a legitimate job? The employment agency had sent her here, explaining that this was a prime job opportunity. Sloane had been told that the company was looking a responsible administrative assistant and receptionist for a new start-up company. Receptionist duties and computer work were tasks that Sloane figured she could handle easily enough. Answering phones? Check, she could do that. Smile and greet people who came to visit? Yep, not a problem. Everything else? Well, she'd survived an illegal eviction after her mother's sudden death, gotten her high school equivalency degree, and convinced a judge that she could support her sisters on her minimum wage, hourly income. That last claim had been an absolute lie, but so far, she'd kept her family together and her two younger sisters were...well, if not thriving, they were together. A family.

As far as Sloane was concerned, anything this Starke guy might throw at her, she could just figure it out, just as she'd done with every other miserable trial life had thrown at her over the past year.

Okay, so she'd have to get the job first.

If this even was a legitimate job. Watching the other women, Sloane was starting to doubt it.

Another woman was called back, the deep voice that called her name was rather intimidating. Sloane shifted in her chair, keeping her skirt demurely over her knees even as the others around her were perfecting their "come-hither" vibe.

Every time that deep voice called another woman back, it seemed as if his bellow was angrier than the last. Impatient bastard, she thought with increasing resentment and fear.

Even worse, she'd been told that her interview time was at two o'clock! She'd switched shifts with another person at the restaurant so that she could be here at two o'clock, thinking that this job was a real opportunity. It was now almost four o'clock! She had to be at work in thirty minutes and she didn't think that her boss would appreciate the excuse that she was interviewing for another job as a good enough reason to be late!

The last beauty sauntered out from behind the wall and the mysterious, deep voice snapped, "Sloane Abbot!"

Sloane stood up, hitching her plastic-wannabe-leather purse higher onto her shoulder. The other candidates had carried leather briefcases, most of them holding an elaborate day planner in their arms. They'd all looked professional and amazing! Sloane felt and looked like a candidate for...nothing. She looked horrible compared to the other beauties this man had interviewed today, but she lifted her chin and stepped behind the wall.

"Sit down!" the tall, terrifyingly large man snapped, rubbing the bridge of his nose and sipped coffee out of a ceramic mug.

Sloane sat on the metal folding chair, perching on the edge as if she knew that she'd be tossed out in a moment. When that happened, she wanted to be ready, although she'd love to come up with some perfectly succinct comment about the tardiness of this interview and how rude he was. He might look like a Greek god, with a sharp jawline that should be in a razor commercial, a head of thick, dark hair and broad, impossibly huge shoulders that pulled at the white material of his dress shirt.

That was about all she could see of the man since he was looking at the papers on the cheap, metal desk. Except for that hand. He had nice hands, she thought. His fingers continued to rub his forehead, not looking up at her. Almost as if he knew she was a fake.

"How fast can you type?" the man demanded.

She once again noticed his broad shoulders and the exhaustion in his voice. The jet back hair was tousled as he tapped his pen against the paper that, she assumed, was her resume. A resume that looked pathetic. It filled only half the page.

4

"About sixty words a minute."

The man opened his mouth to ask the next question, but he froze and actually lifted his head to look at her. "Sixty?"

Sloane wasn't sure if that startled reaction was good or bad. Sixty words a minute seemed pretty fast but...maybe it wasn't? Maybe he needed more.

"And do you take dictation?"

Dictation? What was that? Wasn't that...didn't secretaries from the nineteen forties take dictation? She suspected that was a joke. "No, sir."

His gaze sharpened as he looked her over and she noticed that his eyes were a clear, astonishing green surrounded by thick, almost black lashes. Green eyes? The man seemed too harsh for such pretty eyes. Every part of him screamed "predator" and yet, his eyes with the long, dark lashes, were...there was no other word for it. His eyes were pretty. Beautiful, actually. Set against the taut, tanned skin of his harsh features, the eyes were startling.

Slowly, the man shifted in his chair, the metal squeaking as his long, muscular body unfurled. Like a python, she thought. He leaned his forearms against the ancient desk, those green eyes peering at her through those lashes and Sloane felt a wave of something alarming hit her.

But she wouldn't back down! Not this time! She'd endured the icy cold rain of her mother's funeral, dropping out of high school, living in a shelter, and working twenty hours a day for the past six months! No way was she letting yet another man intimidate her! Not this time!

"You can barely type and you don't know dictation. You seem to be barely out of high school...why the hell should I hire you?" he demanded. "Do you have any skills at all?"

Oh, that was so unfair! Sloane glared at the man, ignoring the danger signals in his "pretty" green eyes. She was sick of men treating her like dirt! Her landlord had kicked them out of their apartment illegally, her boss thought it was okay to grope her whenever he passed by, and her father had ignored her from the moment of conception. Men were... bastards!

"What can I give *you*? Well, let me see!" She stood up, too angry to sit still. "I have patience, since you set up this interview for two o'clock and it is now almost four-thirty. I have determination, because believe me mister, you have no idea what I've gone through over the past six months! And what's more? Hiring me means that you'll get someone who actually *wants* to work! The others out there were looking to jump into your bed. Trust me, several of them were bragging about their chances of bedding you while they waited."

She took a deep breath, and kept going. "What's more? I'm a damn good worker! I *am* barely out of high school, but before I left school, I took over the high school newspaper when no one else would and turned it around. All by myself. I had absolutely no idea how to put a newspaper together, but I figured it out. I also figured out how to do payroll for my current job, run a chicken fryer, and flip burgers. All at the same time! I create the schedules for thirty employees because the manager is too lazy to do it himself. And I've done all of it without training."

She leaned forward, glaring at him. "So, hiring me means that you'll get an employee who might not know everything immediately, but I figure things out. I get the job done correctly and efficiently. Furthermore, I definitely won't be trying to get into your bed! If that's not what you're looking for Mr....whatever your name is, then fine! I'm sick of my boss groping me anyway!"

With that, she stalked out of the building. Thankfully, her car started on the first try and she puttered out of the parking lot, unaware of the tears streaming down her cheeks. It would have been awesome if she could have screeched her tires as she sped out of the parking lot, but this car, and she used that term loosely when referring to the tin can on wheels she was driving, didn't screech. It barely puttered. In this instance, Sloane was just grateful that it didn't putter out and die.

When she was a mile away, Sloane released the breath she'd been holding, trying to shake off the tension from the miserable, wasted afternoon. Another jerk! Another man trying to throw his weight around! Oh how she hated men like that! She hated men in general, but jerks who thought they could control someone else simply because they had money or power, or both, were real assholes! They were gross, disgusting, horrible human beings!

Parking at the fast food place, she reached into the back seat and pulled out her cheap, polyester uniform. For a moment, she contemplated changing in the bathroom versus here in the parking lot. But if she went inside, Sloane wasn't sure that her boss would leave her alone while she changed. She didn't doubt that he'd find a reason to "check the bathroom" while she was in there mid-change. So she figured it was better to risk being seen here in the parking lot than tempting fate, and the pervert, inside.

Parked at the far end of the parking lot, Josh watched as the young woman somehow changed out of the pathetic skirt and blouse she'd worn to the interview and into a pair of jeans and the ugliest striped shirt he'd ever seen. Glancing in the fast food place, he realized that the shirt was the same colors as the tacky décor.

What the hell was he doing here? Yeah, the young woman had struck a nerve back at the interview, but she'd been belligerent and loud. And yet, his instincts told him that Sloane Abbot would make the perfect assistant. Unfortunately, she didn't have the skills he'd advertised, was completely lacking in the confidence that he preferred in his employees, her clothes had been threadbare in several places...but she had guts. Yeah, that was what he was looking for. He needed someone to help him grow his company and Sloane Abbot had gumption. He almost laughed at the antiquated term.

Driving out of the parking lot, he pressed a button on his steering wheel. "Jefferson!" he called out when Jefferson Lamont, his friend and mentor, answered the call, "I'm heading to your place. I'm about to do something stupid."

"Sounds interesting. Come on over," the older man hung up.

Five years ago, Josh might have laughed at Jefferson's abrupt way of handling cell phones. But now it was simply expected. Fifteen minutes later, Josh pulled into the driveway of an enormous house. Some might call it a mansion, but Jefferson would snap at anyone who dared, even though there was a carriage house guarding the front gate, fifteen bedrooms in the main house, and there was even a pool house at the opposite end of the enormous pool.

Spring was a good time to visit this part of the country. Right now, everything was green and lush. In a few more months, the grass would be brown and the trees struggled to hang on to any precipitation. By August, everything would be hot and miserable.

No brown lawn here though. Jefferson had an elaborate sprinkler system that watered everything in the early hours of the morning and the pool sparkled invitingly in the sunshine on those hot, summer afternoons when it was too miserable to do anything but swim. Of course, Jefferson Lamont was what some might call disgustingly rich, but Josh knew him to be an extremely good man. No one knew how generous the old bastard really was. But Josh did. Josh had been a gutter rat, only two steps away from prison when Jefferson had pulled him out of the harsh and unforgiving streets and cleaned him up. Josh owed the old man everything, although no matter how much money Josh made, Jefferson refused to accept repayment.

So, Josh was going to take a chance on someone else. Someone that Josh sensed needed a break, just like the old man had done for him.

"What has your panties in a twist?" Jefferson demanded as soon as Josh entered the library.

Josh tossed Sloane Abbot's resume onto the old man's desk, then walked over to the liquor cabinet and poured himself a scotch, not bothering to ask permission because it would only piss the old man off.

"You're hiring a girl?" Jefferson asked, his white, bushy eyebrows lowering in anger as he looked at Josh, now sitting in one of the chairs in front of the man's desk.

"I'm hiring *me*," Josh countered.

Jefferson let the resume flutter back to his desk as he sipped his scotch. For a moment, he contemplated Josh. "So, who is she?" he asked.

Josh shrugged one massive shoulder dismissively. "I don't know. But she's young, desperate, and on the brink of disaster." He paused, the glass halfway to his mouth as he said, "She might actually have reached disaster and is just muddling through, trying to keep her head above water, although she might be sinking pretty fast."

Jefferson's lips pressed together and he took a long sip of his scotch. "What happened to her?"

Josh stared at the amber liquid in the crystal glass, his eyes narrowed as he thought back to the lovely girl-woman's furious words just prior to her less than epic departure. "I don't know. But she's too damn young to have such an attitude." He paused, smiling for a moment. "You should have seen her, Jefferson. She was...amazing! This Abbot woman...she yelled at me. She told me that the other women who had been in for interviews before her were only trying to get into my bed and I should hire her simply because she's a good worker and because she'd stay well away from any sort of sexual liaison with me. That she was sick of men who manipulated...or something along those lines. She was..." he paused again, shaking his head. "Fabulous."

Jefferson leaned back in his chair, watching the young man who had come so far in life in such a short period of time. Josh Starke was like a son to Jefferson, but it had taken a lot of determination and patience to get him to his current success. And damn if Josh Starke wasn't the epitome of success! Jefferson couldn't be more proud of him if the kid was his own flesh and blood. Unfortunately, Jefferson had never found the kind of love that would make all of his financial success worthwhile. And he'd never taken the time to have a family, something he deeply regretted until meeting Josh Starke one miserable afternoon.

But had Jefferson pushed Josh too far? The man worked hard and was brilliant. He was already ridiculously wealthy and Josh's power would only increase with his latest move to start his own investment firm. Unfortunately, Josh worked twenty hours a day, not bothering to really enjoy life. The same path Jefferson had taken. Josh always enjoyed the ladies, but only for a week or so before moving on. Josh would never find a loving woman if he kept pushing himself to succeed further in business.

Jefferson knew that if Josh weren't careful, then the man would end up just like him. And adopting this girl...he glanced down at the resume again, there was no doubt that she was still a child...might be just what Josh needed. For the past several years, Josh had been so focused on work that he hadn't taken the time to have fun.

Sloane Abbot, huh? He'd have to get his people to investigate her. "Well, what are you doing here then? Why aren't you...?"

"Stop!" Josh laughed. "I came by to ask for a favor."

"What's that?"

The housekeeper knocked on the door, announcing that dinner was ready. "For both of you," she said, turning to Josh with an admonishing look, warning him that he was expected to walk right into the dining room and eat whatever she'd fixed for the two of them. Hell, probably the three of them. Wilma wasn't shy and sometimes sat down and ate with the two men she took such good care of. And Josh didn't have to be a betting man to know that Wilma would sneak a bag of leftovers into his car. She was a mother hen if ever he'd seen one and didn't like that Josh ate at restaurants for most of his meals. She cooked extra for him so that he'd have a home cooked meal at least once a week.

Josh sighed, rubbing the bridge of his nose for a moment. "I recognize the address she put on her resume." His lip curled in disgust. "She's living at the shelter downtown. She mentioned something about...well, she needs a place to live."

Jefferson nodded. "Done. Wilma?" he called out.

Of course, Wilma appeared in the doorway, already nodding her head. She heard all that went on in this house and anticipated her men's needs, usually before they even realized they needed something. "I'll have the carriage house cleaned up and ready for her."

"Thanks," Josh said with deep sincerity. "I don't like the idea of some-one as young and vulnerable as this Ms. Abbot living in a city shelter."

"Agree." Jefferson stood up and walked around his desk, downing the rest of his scotch before Wilma took his glass away. He had a hidden stash of cigars too.

Over dinner, Josh and Jefferson discussed business and went over Josh's next step. By the time he stepped into his car at the end of the night...a huge cotton bag on the passenger seat overflowing with plastic containers filled with meals he could easily pop into the microwave for dinner because Wilma knew that he forgot to eat when he was working ...he was going over everything he'd learned over the last few hours.

So, it was a surprise when he pulled back into the parking lot of the fast food restaurant with the gaudy colors. Even from the parking lot, he could see the smiling face of Sloane Abbot as she greeted a late night customer. He should head home and get some work done, but instead, he remained in the parking spot and started making calls from there, getting his next business step in place. Already, his net worth was in the multiple million dollar range. He'd done that all by himself through shrewd investments. Now, he was ready to expand his investment goals, but needed to hire a staff to get there. His first hire on this next phase of his career was to get a good assistant in place.

Was he making a mistake in hiring someone so young and inexperienced?

Thinking about Jefferson, about how the old man had taken a chance on him, a nobody, a teenage criminal…Josh shook off his doubts about Sloane Abbot. She was young, but the fire in her eyes…it reminded him of how he'd felt all those years ago when Jefferson had miraculously stepped into his life.

Research, he told himself. Pulling out of the parking lot, he headed back to his home. At twenty-five, he preferred a condo to a house, not wanting the hassle of maintaining a yard. Walking through the door, he tossed his keys into the crystal dish in the foyer, then headed through the great room and down the hallway to his office. His condo was spacious, with four bedrooms, a large kitchen, great room, and an office. He didn't need four bedrooms, but figured he'd grow into the space eventually.

He sat down at his computer and logged in, entering the complicated password and the other security measures. Already, he'd fouled several attempts of someone trying to steal the secrets to his financial success. He'd created a security system that guarded the algorithm for his investment strategy and the firewalls he'd put in place rivaled Fort Knox. His strategy worked better than anything anyone had yet developed. When the Dow Jones Index rose by five percentage points, his investment portfolios rose by nine to twelve percentage points. And it was all in the mathematical system he'd created and formatted.

Tonight, he wasn't researching new companies he might invest in. Instead, he researched a certain young woman with startling blue eyes and a hungry anger that caused her pale, too-thin body to radiate with energy and righteous fury. Damn it, she'd been magnificent! He could still hear her haranguing him for the two and a half hour tardiness of her interview and her small hands fisting at her sides when she'd told him that she'd figure out anything that he threw at her. With a chuckle of admiration, he thought about her absolute certainty that she wouldn't ever be in his bed.

That was good because he wanted an assistant, not a lover. Business and pleasure were separate and, by the time the fiercely-determined Sloane Abbot had sat down for her interview, Josh had been completely fed up with women trying to entice him. How could so many mercenary women have heard about his job opening...and how the hell had they all thought that they could simply saunter in and seduce him?

An hour later, Josh wasn't at his computer any longer. He paced the length of his office, furious at what he'd discovered. Sloane wasn't *just* a fast food worker, struggling to find a new job. She'd dropped out of high school after her mother's death to take care of her two younger sisters. What she didn't know was that the courts were about to serve her with papers that would put her sisters into foster care.

Josh didn't know this Abbot girl at all, other than the twenty minute interview this afternoon. But he sensed a strength inside of her, a power that just needed a bit of direction to unleash. Jefferson had given Josh that direction and guidance years ago. It was time to pay that gruff old man back for his kindness and help Sloane Abbot. He'd have to move quickly in order to save her small family...and possibly her pride.

It took about three hours, but by midnight, he finally had everything in place. Tomorrow morning, he'd find Ms. Abbot and, hopefully, she'd accept his help.

Stripping off his clothes that night, he wondered why he was so sure about Sloane. What was it about her that drew him in? She was too young for any sort of romantic inclinations. Not to mention, she'd vehemently announced that she had no sexual interest in him in any way. That was good, he thought, even though something inside of him told him that he was a liar.

Sloane stood in front of the barren building the following morning, her stomach in knots. She'd received the text message early this morning. "Be at the office at eight o'clock, sharp." That's all it had said.

Was she in trouble? Good grief, she probably should have kept her mouth shut yesterday! The man she'd snapped at, he didn't seem like the kind of man who took kindly to a mouthy teenager.

Sloane straightened her shoulders, her chin lifting with that stubborn pride that would one day be her downfall. She had nothing to be proud of right now. At this point, her life was in shambles, she was a high school dropout and she worked at a fast food joint while living out of a homeless shelter, desperately trying to keep her two sisters safe, clothed and fed. But she wouldn't give up! She'd make it somehow and if this guy wanted to yell at her again, well...she'd just walk away. But this morning over a meager breakfast of rehydrated eggs and lukewarm coffee in the shelter dining area, Rayne and Pepper had convinced her to at least meet with the man, both of them certain that it was a second interview.

It probably wasn't, she thought as she put her trembling fingers on the door handle and, with a sigh, pulled open the door.

The lobby area was empty today. No sexy blonds primping or beautiful brunettes unbuttoning their blouses. No clicks of high heeled shoes or wiggling of butts in tight skirts.

It was quiet. Eerily quiet!

Looking around, she wondered if the text had been incorrect. Did she have the wrong time? Was she...?

"You're late!" the sharp voice snapped.

Sloane looked down at her watch. It was eight oh one!

"I'm..."

The man from yesterday, with those beautiful, green eyes and crazy long lashes, walked...prowled...towards her. He wore dark slacks and a crisp, white shirt with the cuffs rolled up, almost as if he were trying to look professional, but there was just too much raw masculine power to be contained by the fabric of his clothes.

"I expect you to be here at eight o'clock every day, ready to work." His green eyes flashed with icy calm as he glared down at her. Yesterday, he'd been sitting in that cold, metal chair so she hadn't realized how tall he was, but wow! He was at least a foot taller than she was and...!

"You'll have a salary and health care, dental and all the benefits, as well as a retirement package. The health care and dental include you and any dependents." His firm lips curled slightly into what she suspected the man might consider a smile, but was really just a baring of his teeth. He leaned forward, "As soon as you set all of that up." With that he turned, leaving her standing in the oddly open space as her mind tried to understand what he'd just said.

Without waiting for her to respond, the jerk moved into the empty space of the building. "I've hired a construction crew, but you'll be in charge of supervising the progress here. I'll be working from my home office and will come by to ensure that progress is happening. We'll work remotely until this office space is built, but you'll need to keep me informed of all of your tasks." He turned to look at her and Sloane realized that she was still standing near the entryway. "Are you scared yet?"

Terrified! But she didn't say that to him. "Not even a little," she replied, her shoulders pulling back unconsciously.

His sharp gaze bored into hers and she wondered what he saw in her.

He was hiring her? But...why? She didn't type fast enough, didn't know dictation, had been outrageously outspoken during the interview and...he still wanted to hire her? He didn't move for a long moment, just...looked at her, as if he could see into her soul. But surely he couldn't see her terror.

Could he?

"Fine. You're not scared. Tell me when you are and we'll go from there." He turned and started walking again and Sloane hurried after him. He kept talking, listing tasks. Sloane hadn't thought to bring a notebook, so she pulled out the cell phone that she and her sisters shared, quickly typing in notes through the e-mail app.

"Got all that?" he asked, stepping through a doorway and she realized that this was a big office with a window out to the back of the building. She glanced around, barely taking anything in.

"Yes. Got it," she said and finished typing before looking up at him. "What else?"

He chuckled and there was something warm and amazing about that sound. She didn't have time to analyze it because he continued with more instructions.

"This will be your office and mine is in here," he said, walking through another door she hadn't realized was there. "It will be your job to protect me from whoever tries to get through to me without an appointment and the annoying swarms that *will* try and get 'just five minutes' of my time." He named a salary that made her gasp. "Believe me, you'll earn every penny of it," he replied. "And your salary will increase as you prove your value to me. Any questions before I go?"

Sloane looked up at him, trying to absorb everything he'd just said. "Um..." she looked around. "Computer?" she asked, feeling pathetic because she and her sisters didn't even have a computer. She used the one at the county library while Rayne and Pepper made do with the school computers.

"Order one," he snapped, his dark eyebrows lowering with impatience. "That's your job, Sloane. If you need something, you order it. If I need something, you order it faster."

His curt, impatient responses made her heart pound with fear that she'd already messed up and she'd only been on the job for...she glanced down at her watch, startled to realize that she'd been here for only five minutes and he'd already given her enough work for the next ten months!

She wouldn't lose this job! The salary alone could get them out of that horrible homeless shelter! She wanted a place with a door and locks, a place where she and her sisters could sleep and not fear that they would be robbed or assaulted. She couldn't lose this job!

"Fine. I'll start in two weeks. I need to give notice at my…"

He didn't roll his eyes at that response, but she could tell that he wanted to. "You work at a fast food restaurant, Sloane. It's not like your boss is the respectable kind of man you owe anything to. You'll start today or you don't start at all."

With that, he grabbed a jacket that had been laid over a metal chair and left the building, leaving Sloane dumbfounded.

He didn't say goodbye or even tell her how she was supposed to start! What in the hell was she supposed to do? She couldn't afford to buy a computer! She had no resources of her own. If she had a credit card, she'd go out and buy one and just pay it off over time but…!

That's when she spotted the folder on the other metal chair in the corner. She hadn't seen it…or anything really…while he was there because he was such a forceful person. But now that she was alone, she could breathe more easily. In in the folder, there was a credit card… with her name on it! Her name and the name of his company. Starke Enterprises. Huh! She flipped it over, wondering if there was a limit on the card. Also in the folder were the employment forms, tax forms and what looked like a legal document. As she skimmed through it, she realized that it was a non-disclosure agreement. A very thick, scary non-disclosure agreement!

What did he think she was going to reveal? She glanced around at the empty building and laughed, shaking her head. "Who am I going to tell?" she chuckled.

Sitting down on the metal chair, she considered her options. She could work for a disgusting, groping slob of a man who shunted all of his responsibilities off on her and didn't give her any of the credit…or she could start figuring out how to build an office environment and, she glanced down at her cell phone with all of the other tasks he'd given her, and earn a living wage.

It was really a no-brainer. She'd work here just long enough to get experience, do the best damn job ever, then leave the bastard hanging, knowing that no one would ever be as good as she was in the role.

With determination, she fished the beaten-up pen out of her purse and filled out the forms. When that was done, she looked around, trying to figure out what to do next. Her next stop was a computer store. Or maybe an office supply store? Both, she thought.

Stepping into her car, she drove down the street to the nearest strip mall. Thankfully, there was an office supply store there that also sold computers. "Perfect!" she whispered, parking her old jalopy.

Stepping into the store, she looked around, immediately overwhelmed by the number of options. "Just one step at a time," she whispered to herself.

"Can I help you?" one of the sales representatives asked as Sloane walked down the row of laptops on display.

She looked up at the guy, noting his acne and greasy hair as well as his bored expression while his gaze swept over her dime-store clothing.

Annoyed at being dismissed as unworthy, Sloane squared her shoulders. "I need a computer with…" and she spouted off her requirements, including extra memory, extra fast processing speed, the ability to enable a hot spot internet connection, and a few other extras. Sloane had originally thought to purchase the bare minimum of computers, just enough to get her started, not wanting to spend another person's money pointlessly. But her instincts took over and Sloane suspected that she'd need the additional processing speed in order to keep up with her new boss.

"I'll also need an ultra-light weight tablet that can hold scheduling software and notes with ease." She'd also need to stock up on office supplies, she thought, but that could wait until after she'd gotten through the tech issues.

As she spoke, the guy's shoulders straightened and his eyes lit up. "Yes ma'am!" he replied, and moved over to one of the highest priced laptops and started explaining the features. Once she'd selected a computer, he brought her to the tablet area and went through the same ritual, asking a lot of questions because she simply wasn't aware of the various options available on a tablet. She figured the only way she was going to learn was to ask, and being shy about her lack of knowledge was pointless. After selecting a tablet, Sloane loaded up her cart with a printer/scanner/fax machine, papers, pens, stapler, and a few other items.

Then she moved towards the cash register. For the first time since stepping into the store, she hesitated, wondering what the spending limit was on the credit card. The cashier rung everything up, then announced her total. "Yikes!" she whispered, unaware she said it out loud. "I don't know the limit on this card, so…?" she shrugged.

The guy looked at her warily, then down at all of the supplies. "I'll need to see a picture ID," he warned.

Sloane understood, but that didn't mean she enjoyed feeling like a criminal. Whipping out her wallet and ignoring her embarrassed cringe when the pleather spine on her wallet ripped just a bit further, the guy compared her name and picture against the name on the credit card. With a nod, he ran the card through the machine while Sloane waited, her breath caught in her lungs as she anticipated seeing "declined" on the little screen.

When "approved" popped up onto the register, Sloane let out that breath slowly, shocked that it had actually worked. She'd just spent over five thousand dollars on office equipment and computer stuff! Dear heaven! She'd never in her life spent that much money!

As Sloane pushed the cart filled with stuff out of the store, she gripped the handle of the metal cart tightly since her knees were about to give out on her. She'd just spent more money than she'd ever made in an entire year! She'd spent more money in one day than...!

"Can I help you ma'am?" the salesperson called out, running out of the store after her.

Sloane looked behind her, surprise in her eyes. "Oh, um...thank you!" she whispered, not sure how to handle someone offering to help her. Help? People didn't really do that, did they? Not in her experience.

"My pleasure," he replied, and she noticed his cheeks turn an interesting shade of pink. She didn't really understand his reaction as she popped the trunk on her car.

"What's all of this for?" he asked, lifting the printer, which was the biggest box and sliding it into her trunk. Unfortunately, Sloane had to push the three boxes of clothes out of the way. Storing their clothes in the trunk of her car was the only way she, Rayne, and Pepper could keep them from being stolen while they lived at the shelter.

"Oh, um...I was just hired by Starke Enterprises," she explained, not sure if that was appropriate or not. Was her position a secret? Good grief, this was all so confusing!

The boy's eyes widened. "Starke? As in Josh Starke?" the guy asked, pausing with the laptop in his hands.

"Um...yes?" she asked, shrugging slightly. "I don't know much about the company yet, but..."

The guy straightened his shoulders, forgetting about the laptop still in his hands. "I'd love to work with that guy! He's a genius! I mean, seriously a genius!"

Sloane blinked, not sure how to respond. "Well, um...I suppose that he's a very smart man." Although, she had absolutely no idea what the guy actually did for a living other than order her around. Which reminded her, she needed to contact her old boss at the restaurant and let him know that she wouldn't be in tonight for her shift. She also needed to give Rayne and Pepper a head's up that she would most likely be working late. She had no idea how long it would take to get all of this stuff set up. Glancing at her watch, she realized that it was after ten o'clock in the morning and she had so much she needed to get done. That list of items he'd given her this morning was long and she wasn't sure how to get some of the tasks accomplished.

Taking the laptop from the guy, she stored it carefully into the trunk of her car. "Thank you so much for your help," she said, glancing at the plastic name tag on his shirt, "Jeff. But I really have a lot to get done. Mr. Starke has a long list of action items for me." She loaded the rest of the supplies, then straightened. "How about if I take your contact information and, if anything comes up that you might be able to help with, I'll give you a call?" she offered.

Jeff flushed with excitement. "That would be awesome!" He pulled out a card and handed it to her. "Anything!" he assured her. "Anything at all!"

Sloane nodded, stuffing the card into her purse. "Thank you for your help, Jeff," she repeated and smiled.

With that, she got back into her car and sighed with relief when the car started up on the first attempt. This morning, she'd had to wiggle some wires under the hood in order to get the engine to turn over. Unfortunately, she wasn't exactly sure which wire-wiggling had helped, but it had finally started. Her morning ritual was to head out fifteen minutes before she needed to leave, just to get this old clunker started.

As she drove out of the parking lot of the computer store, she wondered what it would be like to drive that sleek, black Mercedes coup she'd seen in the parking lot this morning. It had been the only other car there, and it looked just as lethal as its owner.

Since she had the only cell phone between the three of her sisters, Sloane couldn't easily send her sisters any messages. So instead, she drove back to the shelter and left her sisters' a message on the bulletin board, letting them know that she'd be late and that she'd gotten the job. Then she'd driven back to the building and started setting things up. Laptop first, then she'd driven back to the store to get a cable so that she could connect to the internet. "Should have figured that one out," she muttered, hurrying back out of the store.

It was after ten o'clock that night when she finally finished with everything she thought she could accomplish that day and sent an e-mail to her absent boss, giving him an update.

By the time she returned to the shelter, she was hungry and exhausted. She thought about stopping somewhere to get something to eat, knowing that the kitchen at the shelter was closed by now. But since she only had about four hundred dollars in her checking account, the amount she'd earned from her fast food job, she was loathe to spend any of it on something as silly as food. So instead, she'd parked the beat up old car in the back of the parking lot of the shelter and headed inside, looking for her sisters.

She found them curled up on the cots in the corner, doing homework by the light of the streetlight outside the big window. Sloane's heart ached, wishing that she was smarter and faster or older so that she could give them what they needed; shelter, food, and security. Soon, she thought to herself as she wove between the other occupied cots in the large, gym area. Soon they would have enough money to find a small apartment. Even a studio would be nice! They wouldn't have their own bedrooms, but they'd never had that luxury. When her mother had been alive, the three of them had shared a bedroom. But this...a cot in a homeless shelter really was a pretty desperate situation.

She paused, watching her sisters. Rayne was so determined and focused, looking down at her text book for a long moment before writing something in her notebook. Pepper was just as focused, but she had a stronger memory and didn't need to write things down as often. Rayne could read faster, but Pepper remembered everything she read. It was pretty amazing that neither of her sisters had gone down the rebellious route, although Rayne was sixteen going on forty while Pepper had just turned fifteen and acted as if she were ready to tackle the world. Love for her sisters hit her hard and deeply. She loved them, and wanted to do more for both of them.

Even as she watched, Sloane noticed two of the younger men in the room peering over in their direction with a hungry gaze. No way, she thought! Their mother had gotten pregnant every time she'd lowered her guard and trusted a man! There was some sort of weird fertility going on with the women in her family, so no way would Sloane allow some guy to get close to her sisters! The way their luck had been going lately, a guy's sperm could impregnate one of them from across the room!

Okay, that was just stupid and proved that she probably should have stopped for some milk on the way home from the Starke offices. A couple of dollars wouldn't have broken the bank for the three of them.

But it was past ten o'clock now and all she really wanted was sleep. Eight hours of sleep and a comfortable pair of sneakers, she corrected.

Rayne must have sensed her presence because she looked up from her textbook and spotted Sloane. A bright smile lit up her pale features, and Sloane could detect the sparkle from her red hair even across the dimly lit room. Rayne nudged Pepper, who looked up as well, beaming when she spotted Sloane. Both girls jumped up from their cots and rushed over to Sloane who met them halfway. The three of them embraced each other, sobbing quietly.

"You got the job!" Rayne whispered softly because it was quiet time now. "I told you that our luck would change eventually!"

Sloane hugged them tighter, not wanting to acknowledge anything like good luck for fear that she might jinx it.

Pepper kissed Sloane's cheek, hugging her tightly. "I'm so proud of you!" she whispered.

"We're going to be okay," Sloane said, fighting back the tears. Tears hadn't done anything to save them over the past several months, so they were pointless. A waste of energy!

"Shut up!" someone yelled.

All three of them hushed quickly, because any sort of violation of the rules meant that they'd be tossed out onto the street for the night.

"Come on," Sloane whispered and the three of them moved to the small corner space they called "home".

"Go to sleep," she whispered. "We'll talk in the morning."

Rayne and Pepper both nodded, looking warily around at the others, afraid to make noise.

As Sloane stared up at the ceiling that night, she thought about offering up a small prayer of thanks. She might not make it very long with Starke Enterprises, but she'd learn as much as she could along the way! But even as she tried, the prayers wouldn't come. Sloane felt abandoned, as if God had forgotten about her and her sisters. And all of the people here in this shelter! It wasn't just the three of them. There were so many people in this world who needed help. So, where was this God that everyone said was such a solace?

Not here, she thought as she rolled over.

Chapter 2

"Why are we here?" Pepper asked, looking up at the stone house.

Sloane stared up at the adorable house, feeling a pain of disappointment. "I got a note from someone who said they knew of a place to rent that was inexpensive and clean. They also said that this place didn't need a deposit but...!"

"Are you the Abbot sisters?" an older woman asked, coming around the corner of the tree-lined driveway.

Sloane turned around, pushing Pepper and Rayne behind her back. "We're not trespassing," she announced, a belligerent tone in her voice. "We were given the wrong address. We're looking for an apartment to rent and someone told us that this was the place. I'm sorry," she said to the woman, backing up and herding her sisters towards her car. "We'll leave. I didn't mean to intrude."

The woman smiled and waved her hand, chuckling. "You're not trespassing, honey," she said and pulled a set of keys out of her pocket. "You're in the right place. My boss has been trying to rent this old place out for a while now. You're the first people to show interest."

Sloane looked at her sisters, then up at the stone house. It looked like a rustic, old-style cottage, complete with gables and beautiful windows, landscaping and a solid, wood door. They hadn't had a door in... months!

"What is this?" Sloane asked.

Pepper peered out from behind Sloane. "Looks like a house. But... could it be a mushroom?"

Sloane and Rayne both gave their baby sister a glare, which she completely ignored as she laughed at her sarcasm. "Sorry, but that was a really stupid question. It's obviously a house, Sloane."

Granted, Pepper was right. "Okay, so why is it for rent?" she asked.

"And why for such a low price?"

The woman chuckled. "Oh, it's not that big, and it's not on any of the main streets," she explained. "I'm Wilma and I'm the housekeeper up at the main house. This used to be the house for the carriage caretaker," she explained as she unlocked the door and pushed it open. "Now, keep in mind that the ceilings are low and the kitchen hasn't been remodeled. There's no garage so you'll have to park on the side of the house," she warned. "But other than that, there are three small bedrooms and two bathrooms. A kitchen and sitting room."

The Abbot sisters stepped through the arched, doorway and peered into the front room, looking around with huge eyes. The three of them just stood there, overwhelmed.

"You're trying to rent this out for only five hundred dollars?" Rayne whispered, linking her arm with Sloane's. There was a love seat and two club chairs with end tables and lamps. Checkered curtains covered the small windows in the front room. As they moved further into the cottage, eventually separating to look around, Sloane stepped into the kitchen area, admiring the old fashioned appliances, big sink, and shelves in place of cabinets. The counters had curtains that covered the shelves below and there was a small wooden table with four chairs around it. She clicked the switch and the small room filled with light. The walls were yellow and someone had sewn flowered curtains to match. It was an incredibly cheerful room with lots of space, a big window over the sink, and a bigger one beside the table with a door leading out to a tiny backyard.

"What do you think?" the housekeeper asked.

Sloane crossed her arms over her chest, her hands clasping her elbows as she looked around, almost afraid to believe in the possibility of moving into a place like this. Yes, the ceilings were low, but everything was in much better condition than the furniture that they'd lost months ago when their landlord had illegally evicted them. She heard Rayne and Pepper's feet over her head on the next floor and glanced at the older woman.

"I don't..." she wanted to yell out "Yes!" but was afraid. This couldn't be happening, she thought. She'd just gotten a job, an amazing job that paid better than she'd ever thought possible, two days ago. Now someone was offering her a house? A freaking *house*? And the rent was only a fraction of what they'd have to pay if they'd found a small apartment in a commercial building. The three of them had discussed renting a studio apartment because it was cheaper and it would allow them to get out of the shelter faster. But all of the apartment complexes required a month's rent as a security deposit, a cleaning fee, and the first month's rent up front. That was several thousand dollars in this area. Money that they just didn't have yet. Plus, with her last job at the restaurant, she wasn't sure that she could earn enough for a full months' rent on minimum wage, even with Pepper and Rayne working whatever part time jobs they could find.

"What kind of security deposit is required?" she asked, wary and hesitant.

The woman waved her hand again. "Oh, don't worry about that. If anything breaks, just give me a call and I'll get Dennis out here to fix it. We don't need a security deposit."

No security deposit? That was...unheard of!

The woman smiled gently. "Why don't you go look upstairs at the bedrooms and talk it over with your sisters?" she suggested. "I'll wait outside and I can answer any questions you might have."

And with that, the woman let herself out, pulling the heavy door closed behind her with a solid thud.

Slowly, Sloane walked up the narrow stairs. It was small, but there were three actual bedrooms up here. One was a sort of master bedroom with its own bathroom. The other two bedrooms were only slightly smaller, and they shared a bathroom between them. All three rooms had a full sized bed with blankets and pillows, a nightstand, dresser, and lamp. Nothing else, other than curtains on the small windows, but they were quaint and pretty and...so much better than the cots they'd slept on for the past several months!

"What's going on?" she whispered to Rayne and Pepper.

"I know. This feels weird," Rayne said, crossing her arms over her chest. "It's almost too good to be true."

Pepper nodded. "Yeah, this is *too* nice. It's a bit creepy."

Sloane nodded, looking around at the adorable cottage. It was even furnished! "We should get out of here. Something just isn't right."

All three of them nodded, then turned to walk down the stairs. They were so narrow that they had to go down single file, but by the time they reached the front door, they were almost running to get out of the house.

But outside, they came to a stop because a man in his mid-seventies was standing in front of the house, leaning heavily on a cane.

Once again, Sloane pushed Pepper and Rayne behind her, but they tried to step in front of her, each trying to protect the other two. It would have been comical if they hadn't been so terrified.

"I'm Jefferson Lamont," the older man explained, extending his hand to Sloane. "And you are Sloane Abbot." He shook Sloane's hand, then turned to Rayne, shaking her hand and then Pepper's. "It is a pleasure to meet you ladies," he said with a gentlemanly voice. "And this," he said, waving to the older woman standing behind him, "is my house-keeper, Wilma."

"Sir," Sloane said with a nod of acknowledgement. "Thank you for the offer, but we'll have to turn it down."

"Don't," he said softly, looking every moment of his seventy-plus years. "Please, girls, don't turn down my offer." His hands clasped over his cane and he smiled. "I'm a very wealthy man and I have a ridiculously large house, including this carriage house. I know what the three of you have gone through over the past several months, and I guarantee that I don't have any nefarious plans. I just want to help." When he saw the stubborn just of Sloane's chin, he sighed. "You're working for Josh Starke," he said to Sloane. "Is that correct?"

"Yes, but...?"

"He's a good man," Jefferson interrupted gently. "And he said that the three of you needed a place to live." He tilted his head towards the carriage house. "This place has been empty for a while now. Please, take my offer and move in. Today, if possible. You'll be safer here than at the shelter. Josh recommended you," he explained, and smiled as if he grasped a secret. "I think I understand why."

There was a long moment of silence and Sloane could hear the indecision pinging between her and her sisters. "Why?" Sloane finally demanded, asking the question they were all thinking.

Jefferson shifted, standing up slightly and smothering his amusement. "Well, let's just say that I have a sixth sense about people. It's part of the reason for my success, and let's leave it at that, shall we?"

"I don't think...!"

The man frowned unrelentingly at them. "The rent is five hundred dollars, which I will put into a retirement fund for each of you and will ensure that the money is invested properly. The rent is pointless to me, but I invest in people. I suspect that the three of you will go far in this world." He looked directly at Sloane. "Take the house and come up to my place for dinner." With that, he turned around and headed towards the pathway that lead to a line of trees. "I'll expect you at six!" he called over his shoulder, not waiting for an answer.

Wilma waved to them and followed the older man without another word.

Sloane, Pepper, and Rayne watched until the duo disappeared into the woods. Sloane turned to her sisters.

Sighing, she rubbed her forehead, not sure what to do. "What do you think?" Sloane asked.

Rayne stood with her arms folded over her stomach, contemplating the situation. Finally, she nodded firmly and looked at Sloane, then at Pepper. "I trust him," she announced.

Sloane and Pepper stared at Rayne in surprise. "You never trust anyone," Pepper whispered in awe, a slow smile making her blue eyes glow.

"It's settled then," Sloane decided with a firm nod. "We'll live here until we figure out what the catch is." She turned to face her sisters. "But we live frugally, saving up every penny we can! We're not going to be caught without money again!" she told them forcefully.

Pepper and Rayne nodded in full agreement. "We'll all work, earning money however we can," Pepper assured her.

Rayne linked arms with her sisters. "I bet I could get some babysitting jobs around here," she announced, their positive attitudes coming back to give them a small glimmer of hope. Then they moved over to the car and each lugged their box of clothes out of the trunk and up the narrow stairs.

Chapter 3

Sloane pulled into the parking lot early the following morning, looking around warily but not seeing the sleek Mercedes. Breathing a sigh of relief, she shoved against the door of her car. "Ouch!" she muttered, rubbing her shoulder. But for once, the jammed car door didn't bother her. Because for the first time in more than six months, she'd gotten a full eight hours of sleep.

"Mr. Starke, brace yourself!" she whispered as she strode purposely into the building.

Thankfully, keys had been included in that envelope on her first day here, so she could get into the building without him, plus she locked it during the day when she was here alone. Looking around, she bit her lip, trying to determine what needed to get accomplished first. Desks, she thought. Not desks for the whole building, but desks for herself and for her boss. She had a computer now, but needed somewhere to put it!

"You're early!" a voice growled behind her.

Sloane spun around. "Mr. Starke! What are you doing here so early?"

"I'm always here this early and call me Josh. I hate formality. Now explain to me what you're doing here this early."

Sloane pressed her lips together, shifting her feet impatiently. "Yesterday, you told me that I was late when I arrived one minute after eight o'clock. Today, you're angry because I'm early." She started to say something more, but smothered the sarcastic comment. "I'm ready to work. And my first thought is that we need desks." She pulled a notebook out of her purse and pen, which she'd bought yesterday at the office store. "Can you tell me how many employees you anticipate hiring?"

"At least fifty to start. Once they are working efficiently, then I'll expand."

She wrote that down, then looked up at him. "And what's the style of furniture that you'd like for your office?"

"Clean. But hire a decorator to get things in."

She blinked in surprise. "Won't that be expensive?"

He chuckled and something inside of her tightened at the sound. She ignored her reaction and focused on his next words. "I'm a wealthy man, Sloane. And I'm determined to become even wealthier. I'll need to project wealth in order to attract more clients. Also, the kinds of people I want to hire will demand a work environment commensurate with their skills and egos."

She wasn't sure what he meant, but suspected that he planned to hire a bunch of arrogant jerks. But instead of offering her opinion, she wrote that down as well. "Right. Hire a designer." She scribbled quickly, sensing that he was impatient with her questions. "If I'm to oversee the construction of this building, can you give me the name of the contractor you've hired?"

He named the company, and she wrote it down. For the next fifteen minutes, she asked questions and he answered them, if not patiently, at least he answered them thoroughly.

"Any other questions for me?" he asked.

Sloane glanced down at her list, more than slightly intimidated by what he was asking of her. She had no idea how to hire an office designer, but as she looked up into those green eyes of his, eyes that were watching her as if he suspected he'd made a dire mistake in hiring her, Sloane stiffened her resolve. "None, Mr....uh, Josh," she finished lamely.

"Good. Then I'll leave you to it. I'll be working out of my home office. Email me at the end of your day with your progress." With that, he turned and headed towards the exit. With one hand on the door, he paused and turned back to her. "And Sloane, you need to get out of here *before* ten o'clock tonight."

With that, he left and Sloane felt...deflated. There was something about the man that was enervating. And that was such an odd sensation, so she brushed it aside as ridiculous. For the next several hours, she researched and sifted through all of the information. There was a knock on the glass doors around one o'clock and she looked up, startled to see a food delivery person standing at the door, looking around as if he suspected that he was in the wrong place.

Sloane walked over to the door and unlocked it, pushing it open slightly. "Can I help you?" she asked.

The guy jumped at the sound of her voice, then smiled weakly. "I have a delivery for Sloane Abbot. Is that you?" he asked.

She nodded, not sure what to say. "But...I didn't order anything."

He pulled a bag out of his satchel and handed it to her. "Well, this was ordered for you by some guy named Starke. At least, that's what's on the credit card receipt." And a moment later, the guy, barely more than a teenager, hurried away.

Something warm and wonderful blossomed in her chest as she peered into the bag and found a meatball sandwich with chips and a soda. The bag was still warm and she went back inside the building, locking the door behind her.

"Thank you for the sandwich," she e-mailed to him.

In response, he sent her a list of other tasks he wanted her to accomplish. As Sloane looked at the list, she suspected that she could truly grow to hate her green-eyed boss. Seriously hate him!

"I'll make it six months," she vowed. "Just six months and then I'm gone!"

By seven o'clock that night, she'd either finished everything on the list he'd given her this morning or had made headway if the task required others to get back to her, such as researching health insurance options. Feeling extremely proud of herself, she shut down her computer and sighed with satisfaction. Some of the task items had been simple, such as scheduling meetings and arranging for a delivery person to deliver some papers to the lawyer's office. Other tasks had been more complicated and required her to call several people, asking for help. But she'd done it! Sloane had panicked a bit over some of the tasks, not sure even how to figure out how to do them, but she'd called one of the social workers at the shelter who had helped her and her sisters over the past few months, Maggie Bennet. Maggie knew a lot of people and connected Sloane with people who knew other people. Eventually, she'd figured everything out and patted herself on the back.

"You're still working?" he snapped as soon as she called to update him. "Get out of that building, Sloane. Call me in the morning!"

And he'd hung up on her.

Sloane stared at her cell phone, furious with the horrible man and wishing that he were here so that she could kick him.

"Six months!" she muttered as she gathered her belongings and stomped out to her car. "Just six months!"

Josh muttered under his breath as he glared at the phone. "She should have left two hours ago!" he growled, prowling his office, glancing back at the phone every few steps. He wanted to call her, to make sure that she'd left and gotten home safely. But he resisted.

For ten minutes.

In the end, he couldn't banish his concerns for her safety. Sloane

Abbot, he was discovering, was a determined, stubborn woman, who wouldn't stop when it was good for her simply because she was out to prove something to the world and to him.

He understood why, but she was in the building by herself after hours. That wasn't safe!

With a muttered curse, Josh grabbed his keys and hurried out of his building, flinging himself into his car. He broke several speed records along the way to the office. Why he felt so protective of his new assistant, Josh didn't bother to examine. He just needed to make sure that she'd made it home alive, safe and sound. Even her current car was a death trap, he thought and made a mental note to get a mechanic out there to look it over. It was most likely a candidate for the trash heap, but he doubted she would accept a new car from him. He could damn well afford it though, thinking that he just wanted to take care of his employees.

If he looked too closely at his inner thoughts and motivations, he would have understood that his protectiveness wouldn't extend to the employees that he would eventually hire onto his staff. But there was no way he would examine why he felt so protective of Sloane. She was too young and too damn beautiful. Not that he'd paid attention to her appearance. Nope, he hadn't noticed her dark, silky hair or the pale skin that needed significantly more food than she was eating in order to glow. Josh pushed the image of those huge, baby blue eyes out of his mind. He suspected that she wasn't eating well, saving their meager food supplies for her younger sisters. With that in mind, he pressed a button on his steering wheel, activating his cell phone.

Wilma picked up on the first ring. "Hey there, honey. What's going on?"

"Hey Wilma. I was wondering if you might have any leftovers from Jefferson's dinner tonight?"

Wilma laughed, a full-bodied, throaty laugh that pulled a rueful smile from him. "I know where your mind is going and trust me, it's already done, honey," she assured Josh. "I'll be making extra for a while, until those sweet girls get some color back into their cheeks. Especially Sloane. That girl is skinny to the point of being sickly."

"I agree. And, since you brought up Sloane, any chance she's at the house yet?"

"Let me check," he heard her pressing buttons on the security panel. "Yeah, she's pulling through the gate now. What are you doing working that poor girl so hard?"

"I told her to leave two hours ago," he growled. "She's stubborn, Wilma. She just..." he didn't finish, not sure how to describe the woman-girl that he'd hired for no other reason than his gut told him that she'd be a good fit.

"Yeah, but she's a good person," Wilma replied, her voice softer, warmer now.

Josh didn't reply, but nor did he alter his course, heading over to Jefferson's estate even though Wilma had assured him that Sloane had arrived home safely. He still needed to see for himself, and didn't question the reason. He just...needed to make sure she was safe.

He pulled through the gates of his friend's estate and turned down the long, winding driveway, and breathed a bit more easily when he saw Sloane's impressively rusty car parked next to the carriage house. And inside, she hadn't pulled the curtains that Wilma had made for them yet, so he could see the three girls through the windows.

For a long moment, he watched as the girls hugged Sloane, then they worked together to heat up the dinner Wilma had brought them.

As he watched their interactions through the window, he found he could easily distinguish their individual personalities. Rayne frowned a lot, and there was an intensity in her eyes that was frightening in someone so young. He had no idea where her future might lead her, but Rayne would conquer whatever world she chose to enter.

Pepper, as the youngest, should be the most spoiled. But as the three of them sat down together at the small table, it was Pepper who jumped up several times to get something from the kitchen. Pepper was also the most creative of the three, he suspected. Sloane was the protector. Rayne was the cerebral one, and Pepper was the creative sister. Such different personalities and, if he looked closely, the only family resemblance was their impossibly bright, blue eyes. The first time he'd seen Sloane, he'd wondered if she was wearing blue contact lenses. But now that he knew her better, he'd dismissed that possibility. Sloane wouldn't dare spend money on anything so superficial as colored contact lenses.

Even as he watched, his gaze was repeatedly drawn back to Sloane. With fascination, he watched as the three took hands at the table, each smiling and saying something. Pepper and Rayne then dug into the food, obviously famished. But Sloane...deeply introspective Sloane, closed her eyes, almost as if she were offering up a prayer.

With a grunt, Josh turned around, and headed home.

Wilma walked into the library with a cup of tea in each hand. She didn't bother to knock since her friend and employer was expecting her. She handed one of the cups to Jefferson, then sat down across from him at the chess set.

"You were right," she said as she settled in her seat.

Jefferson chuckled. "When it comes to people, when am I ever wrong?"

Wilma rolled her eyes. "Don't be a jerk," she muttered. "He drove all the way over here and sat in front of their house, just watching her."

Jefferson's eyes sparkled with triumph. "They'll be good together," he said softly.

Wilma's eyes softened as she reached for her pawn on the chess board. "Is Sloane and Josh the next step in your evil master plan?"

He threw back his head, laughing at her quip. When his laughter finally died down, he nodded his head and said, "Yeah, I guess they sort of are." Then he turned serious. "He works too hard. You've said so yourself."

"I know," she replied, having had this conversation many times before. "And I agree, the boy seems to be fascinated with her." Josh might be twenty-five years old, but to Wilma and Jefferson, he was still a boy.

"I was worried that he might get caught up in Pepper's charm," Jefferson replied, moving his knight into position on the chessboard. "She's a vivacious little thing, isn't she?"

Wilma countered his move with her castle. "Why not Rayne?"

Jefferson shook his head and moved another pawn. "Nah!" he scoffed. "Rayne is too quietly determined. That red hair of hers is going to get her into trouble with the boys when she actually starts noticing them. But Sloane..." he smiled and leaned back in his chair. "There's a quiet dignity about her that Josh needs. I knew from the first time you mentioned those three girls that Josh would be caught in Sloane's web."

Wilma grunted, taking a sip of her tea. "What ever will you do when you're wrong about someone?" she asked, taking his knight in a swift move.

Jefferson grunted, examining the chess board carefully. "Dunno. Hasn't happened yet."

Chapter 4

Eight Years Later

Sloane stood in the small bedroom and looked around, her gaze lighting on the duvet cover that Pepper had made for her several years ago out of fabric scraps. It was a work of art, she thought. The curtains were the same, not matching, but somehow all the patchwork pieces worked together to form a cozy, warm, welcoming room that soothed her.

"Eight years!" she whispered, shocked. "How could eight years have gone by?" She let her fingers drift over the duvet cover, feeling the edges of the pattern that Pepper had so carefully constructed. "I was only going to be here six months," she whispered to the empty room. "How did six months turned into eight years?" she sniffed, fighting the tears that were never far from the surface lately.

With a sigh, she shook her head, trying to dispel her sadness. This wasn't a day for sadness, she told herself firmly. This was a day to celebrate! Pepper was graduating from college today and Rayne had just received her Master's degree in chemical engineering the week before.

Neither of her sisters knew, but Sloane had also graduated from business school. She'd been taking classes on the weekends and in the evenings, first at the community college and then at the university downtown. It had taken her seven years, but she'd finally earned a business degree. She'd thought about doing the whole graduation-walking thing, but had passed on that. Who would be there? Rayne had graduated at the top of her class and already had a job offer. She'd be heading out to California in a few days where she'd lined up a small apartment for herself. Pepper would go in the opposite direction. Having graduated with honors in her design school, she'd snagged a job with one of the top designers in the busy city. The little brat was heading to New

York City next week and was so excited, she was practically vibrating with it.

For the past eight years, Sloane had watched her two sisters grow and discover themselves, figure out what they wanted to do with their lives. Gone were the days when she wondered how they would find enough food or where they would sleep. Sloane had a hefty bank account balance now and, because of Josh's continuous nagging, she'd allowed him to invest her money as well. Because of his brilliance, Sloane had a healthy nest egg, although she kept a significant sum of money in cash as well. The brutally painful lessons from her past were hard to shake.

"Are you ready, Sloane?" Pepper called up the stairs.

Sloane jerked out of her reverie with a start. "Almost!" she yelled back, then pulled open her dresser drawer and froze. The envelope, which had been sitting in her drawer for eight years, called to her. She didn't need to open it to look at it. She'd read that letter so many times, she had the words memorized. In fact, the paper was starting to fall apart due to the number of times she'd read and re-read the letter.

With a shake of her head, she grabbed the box beside the envelope and pulled it out of the drawer, ignoring the letter. Nostalgia could wait for another day, she told herself as she slipped the pearl necklace and matching earrings on. Josh had given them to her years ago when she'd turned twenty-one and Sloane had worn them to every significant event in her life since. She loved feeling those pearls against her skin and couldn't help the small smile every time she remembered the irritated look on his face that night after he'd handed her the gift and wished her a curt "Happy Birthday".

"Sloane! We need to go!" Pepper called.

Sloane smiled as she carefully closed the wooden box. Grabbing her purse, she moved down the stairs.

"Oh my! You look gorgeous!" Pepper exclaimed. "I knew that rose color would look good on you!"

Sloane laughed, hugging Pepper. "It's a beautiful dress. Thank you for making it for me."

The rose dress truly was lovely, with fluttery sleeves that danced around her shoulders. The V of the neckline was a bit deeper than Sloane preferred, but she vowed not to tug at it. The skirt was more rose colored silk but in a high-low style that made her legs look amazing! She felt good, knowing that her sisters had made it. They'd become important people and were going out into the world to do amazing things! Their miserable past in the homeless shelter was gone, buried, and now, she could look to the future.

At that same moment, a long, elegant limousine pulled up outside of the small cottage.

"What's this?" Sloane groaned, but she already knew.

"Did Josh do this?" Rayne asked, whispering to Pepper and Sloane.

Sure enough, Josh stepped out of the limousine, greeting them with a teasing sparkle to those amazing green eyes of his.

"Ladies, you need to arrive at this shindig in style," he announced.

Rayne laughed, an oddity for her since she was normally so serious and intense. "Josh Starke, you are the sweetest!"

Pepper wasn't nearly so restrained and rushed over to him, throwing her arms around Josh. "You're so awesome!" she gushed, then dove into the back of the limousine.

Rayne turned her head towards the line of trees. "Jefferson and Wilma said they'd be here," she announced, her blue eyes showing her worry. Wilma and Jefferson had aged right along with them and all three sisters took turns checking in on them, doing small things for them, and generally making sure they were okay.

"We're here!" a male voice called as Jefferson came down the stone pathway, leaning a bit more heavily on his cane, but he was smiling and Wilma had her hand looped through his free arm.

All the ladies were wearing dresses designed and created by Pepper and they all looked very romantic. New York City was soon to be awash in romance, Sloane thought with a mental laugh.

Josh laughed softly at Pepper's exuberance, hugging her back as if she were a niece or younger sister. And then Rayne walked over to him, kissing his cheek softly. "You're a good man," she whispered to him.

Sloane watched, waiting for it and bracing herself for his terse response. Over the past eight years, Sloane had learned never to compliment Josh Starke. He didn't take compliments well at all! So it was a surprise when Josh winked at her, then jerked his head towards the limousine. "Get in, brat."

Rayne smiled brightly up at him and stepped into the limousine.

But as soon as he turned those sharp, green eyes towards her, she felt it. The dark eyebrow went up, taunting her, daring her to say anything.

She rolled her eyes and stepped into the car, trying to ignore the horrible man. Why was his gruffness reserved for her? Because she worked for him? Eight years ago, she'd taken that kind of gruff attitude and just ignored it. But slowly, as she'd gained confidence in her abilities to not just handle every task he threw at her, but had started to anticipate his needs, she'd started to fight back. When he was gruff, she simply doled out her own flavor of impertinence. A slight lift of her eyebrow when he was too snippy, or patiently waiting for him to acknowledge her assistance, standing silently until he gave her a curt thank you. At which point, she'd smile brightly and leave him to his grumpy self.

Oh, how she loved tormenting him, forcing him to be polite! It was so much fun! Sometimes, she suspected that he was gruff just to see if she would assert herself. But no, that was silly. Josh was too busy to play games like that. Every moment of his day was a jumbled mess of activities and information coming at him. He seemed to understand everything anyone told him. And not just understand, the man was like a machine! He could take a piece of arbitrary information and anticipate what the markets were going to do because of it. She'd seen him listen to someone at the next table during one of their many meals together, maybe overhearing something about someone ordering a large shipment of ice cubes, and he'd realize that they were going to release a new solar panel into the market. By the time the news came out, he'd already bought shares in the company. Every time he did something like that, Sloane would get a weird tingle in her stomach. She admired the man. Yeah, she admired the hell out of him, although she'd never tell him so! No way!

Shifting over on the leather seats, she smiled as Pepper adjusted the bow on Rayne's dress. Sloane was so damn proud of her sisters! For the past several days, she just kept thinking that one thought. So proud!

Josh watched unblinkingly as Sloane stepped into the limousine. He couldn't stop the stab of lust as he took in the soft, sensual curve of her derriere as she stepped into the vehicle. And the long legs, accentuated by the rose colored heels was like the lick of a flame against his already tormented body. Was this his punishment for being such an ass? Was Sloane doing this on purpose? Did she know that he wanted to toss her over his shoulder and lock her in a bedroom for the next month while his hands and mouth learned all of the secrets of her body?

No, she couldn't know, he told himself firmly. There's no way she could know how he felt about her. At least, he hoped she didn't know.

Hell, Sloane wasn't an idiot. She might know.

That's when he looked up and saw the knowing smirks on his friends' faces. Wilma and Jefferson stood there, silently laughing at him.

"Are you coming with us? Or are you going to stand there looking smug?" he snapped.

Jefferson laughed outright while Wilma chuckled more subtly.

"Oh, we're coming with you, my dear boy," Wilma replied. "I wouldn't miss this night for anything!" and she laughed as she stepped into the limo.

Jefferson waited a moment, looking at Josh with impressively aware eyes. "You gonna do anything about it?" he asked in a voice that only the two of them could hear.

"No. Get in and be quiet."

Jefferson snickered and stepped into the limousine.

Josh rested one hand on the hood of the vehicle and took a bracing breath. "You did this to yourself," he muttered, then ducked into the dark interior, joining the raucous group. His eyes skimmed over Pepper and Rayne, glad that they were both so excited about the day. But his gaze rested on Sloane. She looked so damned beautiful in that dress. All the fluttering ruffles moved with every shift of her slender body. She was so innocently sensual that it was hard to keep his body from revealing his thoughts. Yes, he wanted to give Pepper and Rayne a fabulous weekend. And the limousine was only the first thing he had planned to celebrate all three of their successes. And yeah, he knew that it wasn't just Pepper's and Rayne's graduations. He'd seen Sloane studying too many times over the years not to know what she was up to. Damn, he was so proud of her!

How many times had she come to him, asking him questions about one subject or another? He almost laughed out loud every time she tried to trick him into helping her understand a business concept. And every time she'd walked out of his office with that glow of happy comprehension on her beautiful features, as she practically danced back to her desk. Too many times, he thought. Too many times over the past several years he'd watched, helped, and coached her. He wanted her so damn much but...she was oblivious. And he continued to remember her vow that first day, that assurance that she'd never want anything more from him than a job.

She was cute and sexy, innocent and so damned glorious that he had to grit his teeth to keep his body from reacting. A glance at Wilma and Jefferson warned him that he wasn't being as subtle as he'd like.

When he glanced back at Sloane, she was watching him. For a long moment, he looked right back at her, willing her to understand, but, at the same time, praying that she didn't.

That's when he caught it! The blush! His eyes narrowed and his body tightened painfully. But...surely she hadn't...had she?

Oh, hell no! Sure enough, there it was. She'd just blushed! It hadn't been a trick of the light! What did that mean?

A peek at Jefferson told him that he'd seen the look too. On any other woman, Josh would have pulled her over onto his lap and kissed her.

But this was Sloane! Delicate, vulnerable, proud Sloane! He couldn't...surely she didn't...!

He looked over at Jefferson again. The old man just leaned back against the leather cushions of the limousine, looking smug. Had he...? Did he...?

A slight nod of Jefferson's head answered Josh's unspoken question.

Josh was unaware of the muscle twitching in his jaw, but Sloane glanced over, her eyes narrowing as she took in the tension of his body. With focused attention, Josh forced his muscles to relax, not wanting anything to mar this day for Sloane. She deserved this moment of happiness after the past several years. She'd done a damn fine job with her sisters, plus getting herself through college, teaching herself how to do everything he'd thrown at her. He still had no idea how she'd figured it all out. There had been several times, moments of lust-induced insanity when he'd given her seemingly impossible tasks with the hope that she'd resign. He wasn't a total bastard. He would have ensured that she'd gotten another job with a good company.

Yeah, he was fully aware that he could have easily transferred Sloane to a different position. Some job where he wouldn't see her every day, hear the soft, lilt of her voice and smell the flowery perfume she always wore.

His only excuse was that he was insane. Completely insane caused by the ever present need to make love to one of the most gloriously beautiful, alluring, enticing women he'd ever met.

But he'd always come to his senses, not trusting anyone else to treat her with the respect she more than deserved. Yeah, there was a good bit of irony in his logic.

Insanity.

Chapter 5

Sloane stood in the audience, clapping until her hands stung as Pepper walked across the stage to receive her degree. Rayne stood on the other side of Jefferson and Wilma and was jumping up and down, which was completely out of character for her. But Pepper had done the same when Rayne had walked across the stage to receive her master's degree last week, so perhaps Rayne was just giving Pepper a bit of payback.

Unaware of the tears streaming down her cheeks, she stood stiffly, afraid that any sort of movement beyond clapping would shatter her. Pepper had done it! She'd earned her degree and had a wonderful job. But she'd be leaving Sloane...very soon. They'd only see each other occasionally instead of...well okay, they didn't see each other all that often now. Not with everyone's work schedule. But at the end of the day, Sloane knew that her sisters were sleeping at the cottage. They were all under the same roof. In the mornings, Sloane could hear her sisters moving around, getting ready for school or their jobs, maybe heading out for a study session with their classmates or meeting up with friends for coffee, which was rare because they worked so hard. If they weren't working, they were studying, writing a paper, or preparing for the next exam. If they weren't doing any of that, they were at work. But they found time to eat together at least once a week.

That would end now. Rayne would be in California and Pepper in New York. They were adults and would scatter to start their new lives.

"Sloane!" Josh growled. A moment later, Sloane was pulled against his hard body, his strong arms wrapping around her and she didn't have the strength to pull away, to tell him that this wasn't appropriate. There had been tense moments over the years when one or the other would accidentally touch, but after a long, startled glance, they would step back, putting space between them as if the other person was on fire.

This...this was different. Right now, she couldn't put any space between herself and Josh. She needed his strength. In a moment, she'd find her strength again. She'd be strong and competent. She would smile and clap and her dignity would return. But at this moment, knowing that her wonderful, amazing sisters were moving on, that this was basically the end of their sisterhood together, she couldn't help but be so proud and so painfully sad!

So instead of pulling away and finding her dignity on her own, she pressed her face against his chest and absorbed every ounce of understanding she could. She let it all out, releasing everything she'd been trying to control for the past several months in anticipation of this day.

And after the tidal wave of emotions abated, she remained in the circle of his arms, her cheek resting against his chest, listening to the steady thud of his heart. Once again, Sloane told herself to pull away but... she stood there for another moment, selfishly enjoying the feeling of his arms around her. She wanted to snuggle closer, to press her face against his bare...!

Bare what, she mentally gasped. Bare chest? Bare neck? Bare...nothing! Her thoughts had gone rogue.

"Thank you," she whispered, finally finding the strength to pull away. Wiping the tears away, she breathed in and released the breath slowly. Looking around, she suddenly realized that she was actually sitting on his lap!

"Oh, good grief!" she gasped and stood up. "I'm so sorry!"

Josh stood as well, those green eyes of his, for once, not filled with grumpy frustration or teasing amusement. "Feel better?" he asked softly, his voice rough and several octaves lower than normal.

She nodded, still wiping at her wet cheeks. "Yes. That was silly of me," she told him, looking around. "Um...where is everyone?" she asked.

The auditorium was basically empty, the rest of spectators having filed out of the area to meet up with their graduate and re-congratulate them. There were a few stragglers, but they weren't part of her immediate family. "Where are Rayne and Jefferson? Wilma?"

"They went to meet Pepper," he explained, his voice low and grumbly.

"Oh. Well," Sloane wasn't sure what to say to that. "How long did I cry?" she asked, feeling painfully awkward.

He shrugged and looked around, seeming to look for a clock or some other gauge that would give him an indication of time, even though he wore a one hundred thousand dollar watch on his wrist. When he looked back at her, he didn't seem to care about the time, looking down at her with a sort of veiled concern. It was almost as if he didn't want her to know that he cared. "I suspect that you've been holding that in for a while now." He shoved his hands into his pockets and glanced at the exit. "Do you want to go meet your sister now? Or do you need another minute?"

She sighed, feeling silly for her outburst. "I probably need to repair my makeup. I must look like a raccoon."

Sloane looked up at him, praying that he wouldn't tease her. Normally, she could take it. Most of the time, she secretly enjoyed his gruff responses. But not today. She felt too vulnerable right now. It would take her a bit of time to get her armor back in place.

"You look lovely, as always," he assured her. "Come on." He took her elbow, guiding her up the stairs to the exit. "Let's go find the others. We have big plans for this weekend."

His words caught her attention. She watched him warily for a moment, trying to discern his intentions. That's when she saw it! He'd done something extravagant! Again! "What did you do?" she demanded.

Josh was a very wealthy man, having exceeded his goals many times over. He was one of the youngest billionaires in the country, and also one of the most generous men she'd ever met. He'd tried to buy her a car several years ago, but she'd put her foot down until he bought a "company car" and ordered her to drive it. "That death trap you call a vehicle is bad for my company's image, Sloane!"

He'd increased her salary so many times over the years, despite her assurances that she felt well compensated. When they traveled for business meetings around the world, she'd often find small gifts on her bed or he'd just toss a box to her, casually saying that he'd seen something in a window that he thought she might like.

Of course, those small gifts were really outrageously expensive shoes or a dress that she might have silently admired or a piece of jewelry she'd glanced at as they'd walked along the street from one meeting to another.

He often bought Rayne and Pepper presents too. Smaller gifts, things that a big brother might buy for his little sisters. For Pepper's sixteenth birthday, which Wilma had insisted on cooking a fabulous dinner, Josh had casually given Pepper a pearl necklace and pearl earrings. For Rayne's eighteenth birthday, he'd tossed her a small box containing a gold necklace with a locket. Both gifts had been casually given, but at the time, Sloane suspected that Josh put a great deal of thought into the gifts.

And it had warmed Sloane's heart to see the secret joy in his eyes when her sisters wore their jewelry. There had been smaller gifts, cashmere sweaters and wool coats, specialty glass earrings and bracelets... things that Josh could pass off as something he'd "just seen in passing". It was almost as if the man didn't want anyone to know that he cared. It might ruin his image as a gruff, mean billionaire.

Josh would buy Sloane things more often if she'd allow it, but she knew when he was about to do something outrageous and had stopped him in the past. Finally, he'd resorted to just giving her outrageous bonuses.

And he had that mischievous look in his eyes now. Josh Starke was about to do something outrageous!

His green eyes sparkled with amusement as he looked down at her. "Why do you ask like that?"

He was too close and Sloane breathed in the spicy, masculine scent of him, wanting to close her eyes and savor that scent. But she knew that would be a huge giveaway, so she looked him directly in the eye.

"What way?" she asked, curious and stepping back, silently admonishing herself.

"That way that tells me you think you have any say in what I do next?" he replied, chuckling softly as he put a hand to the small of her back to lead her over to where Jefferson and Wilma stood by one of the windows.

"Rayne went to find Pepper," Wilma announced. Then she turned to Sloane. "You doing okay, sweetie? That was a lot of emotion you let out earlier."

Sloane glanced warily up at Josh, wanting her blip of dignity to be banished from everyone's minds. "Yes. I apologize. It won't happen again."

Wilma chuckled. "Oh yeah it will. Just wait until Pepper and Rayne get..." she caught herself, beaming at Sloane. "Never mind. You're going to have a blast this weekend. Promise!"

Slowly, Sloane turned her blue eyes up to clash with his green ones. But as usual, when Josh didn't want to reveal something, there was no way anyone was getting a secret out of him.

"What did you...?" She started to ask, but he touched her arm.

"Relax, Sloane," he ordered gently, his eyes moving over her features softly, as if caressing her. Sloane's hand reacted, flying up to her cheek as if she could somehow cover the blush. "I'm in charge this weekend. You're going to accept it, enjoy yourself, and spend some quality time with your sisters."

She wanted to yell as frustration swamped her, but this was Josh. She knew that he'd never do anything to hurt her or her sisters. Just the opposite, in fact. He went out of his way to ensure their safety. For

Rayne and Pepper, he acted like a big brother. Josh always stepped in when Rayne or Pepper needed help with anything.

"Fine," she huffed, turning to look at the crowd because looking at him made her stomach tighten. She hated that sensation and seemed to be feeling it more often lately. Josh Starke was just so...enigmatic? Yes, but it was more than that. There was something about him, something special, something that made him almost untouchable and unreachable, but at the same time, he knew how to come across as persuasive and approachable.

What was it about him that constantly fascinated her?

"Did you see me?" Pepper called out, rushing through the crowd. Pepper was so outrageously vivacious and gloriously beautiful that the crowds parted for her, heads turning to watch admiringly as she passed. It was the same with Rayne, probably because her hair was so eye-catching, not to mention the quiet intensity that surrounded her. People automatically respected Rayne.

Sloane watched, amazed at the similar reactions caused by seemingly opposite personalities.

In the end, she didn't really care why people were so mesmerized by her sisters, she just cared that her sisters were treated with respect. Sloane loved them because they were warm, wonderful people. She opened her arms for Pepper who, of course, threw herself into Sloane's arms, as she laughed excitedly with her precious degree clutched in her hand.

"We did it, Sloane!" Pepper whispered, literally bouncing with her exuberance.

Sloane laughed and cried, then spotted Rayne right behind Pepper. Immediately, she opened her arms and Rayne moved in to hug her. The three of them laughed and cried as they hugged, a trio celebrating their triumphs. "You both did it!" Sloane said with an urgency that conveyed her intense love for these two amazing women.

None of the laughing, sobbing, hugging women were aware of the glowers from their dark protector as Josh glared at several men who watched the trio, entranced by their beauty. Nor was Josh aware of Jefferson and Wilma standing off to the side, watching smugly.

Chapter 6

"Where are we going?" Sloane demanded, glaring up at him.

"Celebrating," he announced without changing his expression, obviously amused.

There was a huff of impatience. "Yes, but *where*?" she urged with a heavy dose of exasperation.

He shrugged, the dark suit shifting on his tall, muscular frame. "You'll have to be patient and find out."

She fidgeted in the soft leather seat, making Josh chuckle faintly. He knew she hadn't given up on trying to discover his intentions. Sloane never gave up. She might strategically retreat, only to come at him – or any problem – in a different way. But she never gave up.

"You're doing that on purpose, aren't you?" Pepper asked, her eyes pinging back and forth between Sloane and Josh. The four of them were alone in the back of the limousine, Jefferson and Wilma having gone home after the elaborate dinner. "You know that Sloane not only has to know everything, she has to be in control too."

Rayne laughed softly, her eyes moving back and forth between the two of them as well. "They play this game just to annoy each other, don't they?" she said in a mock whisper.

"I think so!" Pepper replied, in an equally theatric voice.

Josh simply lifted a dark eyebrow in their direction. And because they thought of him as a big, sometimes-overly protective brother, they giggled and settled back against the leather seats of the limousine.

All of them were tired after the long, emotionally draining day.

Sloane shifted again, angling her shoulders to glare at him more effectively. "Look, I'm sure that whatever you have planned is lovely, but I'd like to get some sleep."

"You'll get plenty of sleep. Just..." he paused when the driver pulled through the gates of the airport. "We're here," he announced without finishing his previous sentence.

"Here?" Sloane asked, peering out of the windows. "Why are we at the airport?"

"We're taking a flight," he said as if that was the most obvious thing in the world. "You've been here plenty of times before," he admonished. "You should know the routine by now."

It was true that she'd flown with him many times over the past eight years. In the beginning, when he was still working to build up his investment company, they'd flown by commercial airlines, although he demanded that she book both of them in the first class cabin. The first time she'd booked a flight for the two of them, she'd booked him a seat in first class, but she'd taken a seat in the economy class, thinking to save him money. Boy, he'd been livid after that flight and ordered her to never do that again. He ordered her to sit next to him during the flights so that they could work together, although he usually sat beside her silently studying data or reading reports.

But about six years ago, he'd told her to buy a private jet for their travels. She'd been flabbergasted, and hadn't realized that he was serious. It had taken several more conversations with him to convince her that he was serious. So now he traveled in the even more exclusive realm of personal flights and had hired his own pilot and co-pilot, both of which earned a great deal of flight time in his employ.

Peering out the window, she saw that the flight attendant was standing beside the stairs, chatting casually with the pilot as they waited for the limousine to pull up. "What did you do?" she hissed, almost afraid of the answer.

"No way!" Pepper exclaimed, her eyes wide with excitement as she realized they were finally flying on Josh's private jet.

Rayne's response was less vocal, but no less surprised. "Are we really...?" she asked, trying to be polite as she leaned forward, peering out the window.

The driver pulled to a stop right in front of the stairs that had been pushed up against the jet and Pepper and Rayne jumped out, eager for their next adventure.

Sloane lingered in the limousine, shaking her head. "This is too much, Josh!" she hissed, furious with him for spending so much money. And touched.

He stepped out, and ducked down to look back in at her, laughing at Sloane's mulish expression. "Get on the plane, Sloane," he ordered in a smooth, patient voice.

She stepped out of the limousine, shaking her head. "You're outrageous! The dinner and limousine were extravagant enough. Anything more is out of the question!"

Josh turned his head, looking over as Rayne and Pepper practically danced over to the short flight of stairs before disappearing into the luxurious cabin of the plane.

"Sloane, I'm taking your sisters to celebrate this monumental milestone. You can either get on the plane and come with us, and celebrate your own success, by the way, or the driver will take you back to your house. It's your choice. I just thought," he paused slightly, "that you'd like to be around to protect your younger sisters as they travel this weekend."

She held her breath, her thoughts warring with her innate frugality and her innate need to protect her sisters by being by their side. "Fine!" she muttered angrily. "But you're in big trouble!" she warned, then turned and stalked onto the plane. The flight attendant had already handed Pepper and Rayne glasses of champagne.

But Sloane didn't want to be the wet blanket. Her sisters had both graduated and, on Monday morning, would start their new jobs. What harm could one outrageous weekend do?

The flight attendant handed out blankets as the plane leveled off after takeoff. And since they'd all had a crazy day, filled with laughter, tears, and unexpected emotions, they quickly nodded off. Sloane showed them how to extend their chairs for sleeping, and pulled the blanket over her legs, slipping off her shoes and trying to rest herself.

Josh had gone into the private bedroom in the back soon after the plane took off. She knew that he'd probably make several phone calls and tried to keep her eyes open, just in case he needed her. But he didn't call out to her. She snuggled deeper into the lush cushions of the chair, trying to fall asleep because she was truly exhausted. But something kept niggling at her, although, she couldn't quite put her finger on it. Josh had said something. Something important. Her eyes drifted closed in the dim light of the cabin and the soft, smooth sounds of the plane's engines lulled her even more. Eventually, her exhaustion won out and she fell into a deep, dreamless sleep.

Chapter 7

Monaco! Josh had flown the three of them to Monaco!

She glared at him as the limousine drove through the bustling, sunny streets of the glamorous city, eventually pulling up to one of the most exclusive resorts in the entire city.

In flawless French, Josh checked them into the suite, the hotel staff almost tripping over themselves to accommodate the four of them. Sloane had seen it all before and had to control the urge to roll her eyes. It was always like this when they traveled and she wanted to laugh. Her face softened as she looked at Pepper and Rayne. They stood off to the side, their eyes wide as they took in the almost unbelievable luxury. They were actually leaning into each other, as if they needed the support while their heads swiveled around.

"This way," Josh called as two bellhops pushed the carts containing their luggage. That had been a surprise, she'd thought, but then realized that Wilma had probably been in on the whole thing and had conspired with Josh to pack for them.

The bellhop led them to a private elevator, which took them up to the top floor. She knew what would happen next and wasn't disappointed. Josh never stayed in anything less than the best, so when the bellhop pushed open the massive doors to the suite, she just sighed and mentally shook her head.

There wasn't just a sitting room. There was a massive living room, complete with stunning views looking out over the trees to reveal the azure ocean beyond. Upstairs was the master bedroom, and Josh would take that room, she knew. The bellhops efficiently carried the bags to the three other bedrooms, two on one side of the living room and the other bedroom upstairs on the opposite side of the master bedroom.

Sloane took the upstairs bedroom, knowing that Josh usually worked late most nights. It would be easier if she were close by so they wouldn't disturb Pepper or Rayne during these sometimes exhausting work sessions.

Stepping over the threshold, she kicked off her heels and let her feet sink into the thick, luxurious carpeting. The bedroom alone was bigger than their entire house and even had a private balcony with a set of...oh my! This balcony was shared with the master bedroom and she glanced over at the other sliding glass doors. She didn't want to see Josh just now, since she felt a bit vulnerable still. Sloane wasn't sure what that was all about, since she prided herself on always being available for Josh.

She still hadn't figured out what that niggling issue was from the previous night. He'd said something or she'd seen a look from him... something she couldn't put her finger on, but she knew was vitally important.

Oddly, Josh didn't work that day. Instead, he told them to change into something comfortable for walking and being in the sunshine. When they stepped back out of the hotel, they were met by yet another limousine that took them to Jardin Exotique de Monaco. Sloane wondered why he was taking them to a garden, but as soon as they stepped into the mountainside exhibits, she understood. The massive cacti and exotic plants were...shockingly beautiful. Plus, the whole garden was set up high so that they could look out at the harbor filled with beautiful yachts. One in particular was impressively larger than the others.

"I wonder who owns that one!" Pepper sighed, looking out at everything and taking it all in.

"Eh, it's just a big boat," Rayne replied, not overly impressed by the yacht. As a scientist, she was much more interested in the flora and fauna, bending down to read the explanations, only asking Josh to translate a few of the words.

Pepper and Rayne had moved further ahead and Sloane was admiring the view when Josh stepped up next to her.

"How did you learn to speak French so beautifully?" she asked.

He shrugged. "The same way I learned Spanish and Arabic," he said as if he was talking about learning to slice bread. "I just studied verbs and listened to others speak it."

She wondered if that was all there was to it, but decided in that moment that she was going to learn foreign languages as well. And why not? She'd just graduated from college with a business degree, although not from one of the prestigious schools, but she'd done it. Why not keep on learning?

"Don't languages help one to see the world differently?" she asked, fascinated, but trying to hide it. She didn't want him to know how amazing she thought he was, or how many times she'd accidentally found herself fantasizing about kissing him. That was wrong in so many ways that she couldn't even count them.

They talked about learning languages and various other topics as they walked side by side along the pathway. And for once, he wasn't grumpy and demanding, she thought with a wave of happiness.

She was only happy because of how happy he'd made Rayne and Pepper, she told herself, keeping her hands behind her back so that she wouldn't accidentally brush his arm while they walked among the exotic plants.

It was a beautifully relaxing afternoon and she was fully prepared to either work that evening, or curl up on that big bed in her room with a book to quietly enjoying her evening.

But Josh had other plans.

Chapter 8

"I'm not doing it!" she declared with absolute resoluteness.

Josh stared down at her, toying with the square casino chips. "Why not?"

She looked around at the golden lights and the red décor. It wasn't nearly as tacky as she might have thought. This casino was elegant and refined. The low hum of conversation was the perfect backdrop to the classical music playing from discreet speakers as beautiful women dressed in shimmering gowns walked alongside men in tuxedos. Everyone seemed to be drinking sophisticated cocktails or sparkling champagne.

Pepper had literally squealed with delight when Josh had handed out the gambling chips, telling her to have fun. Rayne had stared at the chips with her normal intensity, then lifted her blue eyes to smile politely at him, but with a sincerity that could never be contrived. "Thank you," she'd whispered, glowing with quiet happiness, and followed Pepper's exuberant trail towards the tables.

Sloane was the only one that didn't want to gamble.

"Because gambling gives me an upset stomach."

"It's only a few dollars," he pointed out, reaching out and taking her wrist, pulling her hand forward. With his touch, he saw something in her eyes, a flash of...awareness? He wasn't sure. She started to pull away, but his fingers tightened around her wrist. With his touch, the moment expanded, tension flared. Awareness roared around them and he could have sworn that she felt it as well.

Josh almost asked if she felt it, but someone bumped his arm and he looked around, ready to punch whoever had disrupted them. It took a moment for him to get his thoughts back under control. When he looked back at Sloane, she looked just as dazed as he felt. Unfortunately, the moment was gone and he couldn't ask her…anything.

"Come with me," he told her firmly. "I don't trust you to have a good time on your own."

She huffed a bit and Josh smothered his amusement. It was so typical and he loved that about Sloane. She was determined and dedicated, but also predictable. It was one of the small joys in his life when he threw off her routines and he got to see her luminous blue eyes flare with irritation. Or when he got too gruff with her and she waited, those eyes boring into him. He loved it when she demanded he say "please" and "thank you". There was just something so damned sexy when she tapped her foot impatiently, waiting for him to behave.

"I'm not gambling," she repeated firmly.

"Sloane, you watch me gamble with billions of dollars every day. What's so different about a few dollars at a casino?"

She shifted and he pulled her closer as they made their way through the glamorous crowds. "First of all, you *never* gamble when investing money. You and I both know that everything you do is perfectly calculated." She shifted to pass an overly excited couple that had just won at the roulette table, but the woman unexpectedly threw her hands in the air. Josh pulled her closer, feeling Sloane's soft body press against his for a brief moment. Quickly, she stepped back, glancing up at him nervously as she put more space between them.

"And secondly," she continued, "I don't believe that the chips in your hand represent only a few dollars." She frowned at him. "How much money are you holding in your hand, Josh?"

He smiled down at her, pulling her close again as another couple passed them. "Enough," was all he would tell her. "Relax, Sloane. Think of this as a business adventure. I'm ordering you to figure out how to gamble."

Predictably, Sloane rolled her eyes. "No," she replied firmly.

He laughed, wanting to pull her close and hug her. What would she do, he wondered?

"Why does it bother you so much?" he asked. "It's just money."

Sloane turned and looked up at him. "To *you*, it's just money. But to me, it's more than that. Its security and shelter. It's power."

He tilted his head slightly. "If you're so sure that money can provide those things for you, why haven't you married one of the rich men you've met over the years?" he asked. He didn't add, "Why don't you marry me?" Because…well, because…he wasn't the marrying kind? Of course, if it were Sloane then…!

"Because I refuse to rely on any man for my security and shelter," she replied stiffly.

"That's admirable, but there are many women who would disagree with you."

She shrugged. "Everyone chooses their own path," she replied, looking around curiously. "I just think that I'm safer, and my sisters are safer, if we ensure our own security."

He liked that about her. Hell, he liked a lot of things about her! Too many things, actually.

"Okay, so why not gambling?" he probed.

She looked around, appreciating the splendor of the elegant casino, but he knew that she was holding herself separate from all of it. She isolated herself, even from her sisters sometimes.

"Because it's basically throwing money away, something I'm morally opposed to doing."

He grinned, thinking that she was magnificent. "Okay, fine. Then you can watch me throw my money away. Let's play."

She shook her head, trying to push his hand away when he tried again to offer her some chips. "Nope. You're on your own."

He grinned and shook his head, then leaned in close to whisper in her ear. "You don't really believe that I'm going to lose, do you?"

He felt her shiver. Interesting, he thought as his body reacted. Very interesting!

Sloane's lashes fluttered for a moment before she replied, "Um…it's your money. You do what you want with it."

She folded her hands in front of her, trying to appear demure. But his eyes caught the sparkle of challenge. Challenge issued, he thought. And accepted.

"Let's go," he said, wrapping an arm around her waist to lead her over to the roulette wheel. "Here," he said, forcing a chip into her hand. "Put this on the number you like best."

"Nope," she replied, trying to hand the chip back to him. "You do it. I don't want to be responsible for you losing whatever that amount of money this might be.'

He chuckled, and kept his arm around her waist as he leaned forward, placing his chip on a number. Because he was basically wrapped around her, he didn't even notice which number. When he was touching her like this, he didn't care what he was doing, as long as he could keep touching her.

Sloane gritted her teeth, trying not to make a noise that might alert him about how she felt when he touched her. She couldn't let him know, couldn't reveal her true feelings. Especially when she wasn't sure what her true feelings were. She hated that she shivered every time he touched her. But that didn't really mean anything. She was just cold. Yep, that's it. She was cold and he was warm. That sounded like a good enough excuse, she thought. The sleeveless black, crepe dress was simple and elegant, but it didn't keep her warm. While Josh was hard packed muscles that emanated enormous amounts of body heat.

He moved back, standing behind her and, because of the crowd surrounding the roulette table, she could feel his body press against hers. Someone nudged her, trying to get a closer look as the ball bounced around the roulette wheel and Sloane moved closer to Josh. He understood what was going on and wrapped his arm around her waist again. She looked up at him, but he was watching the roulette wheel and she told herself that his touch was only because of the crowd. He was simply being protective. Yes, that was all it was, she thought. But even as she thought it, Sloane leaned closer and felt his hand tighten on her waist. It felt wonderful, she thought and pretended, for just a moment, that they were a couple instead of just employer and employee. It was an innocent fantasy, she told herself.

And it felt incredibly good!

Chapter 9

Sloane sighed as she stabbed another breaded, sauce-covered piece of shrimp, closing her eyes as the sweet and sour sauce hit her starving taste buds. "Oh, this is so good!" she sighed. "I don't care that Rayne and Pepper get to sit down by the pool while you make me work, as long as you feed me."

Josh groaned, shaking his head as he grabbed another piece of broccoli with his chopsticks. "I don't know how you can eat that stuff," he grumbled, as he pressed a few more keys on his computer. "But I'm grateful for your help, so eat away. Trevitech stocks went down twenty percent because of their last product launch."

Sloane smiled down at her plate. Josh, in tune with every aspect of her personality, caught the flash of amusement. "What?"

She looked back up at him, startled by his question. "What?"

He waved his chopsticks at her. "You made a face."

Her eyes widened in feigned innocence. "I made no face."

"You did. What was the face for?"

She laughed, looking down at her unhealthy but delicious Chinese food. "You're imagining things."

He leaned back, watching her closely with those scary green eyes of his. Those eyes saw everything. Sloane was just tired and punchy enough that she didn't care.

"I'm not. I never imagine. What was that look?" he demanded, taking another piece of steamed broccoli.

She shrugged, put her chopsticks down, and flipped the page on her report. "Six months ago, you predicted that Trivitech would go down by nineteen percent because of their current product launch."

He nodded slowly. "And?"

She grinned, not bothering to lift her eyes again. "And...you were wrong."

There was a long silence as he contemplated her smug expression. His initial instinct was to pull her over his knee and spank her for being so smug. And impertinent. But damn, he loved her teasing tone. She was usually so serious and business-like. Yeah, he admired the hell out of her for her work ethic, but...well, he *liked* her.

Not that he would do anything about his attraction to her. First of all, he remembered his interview with her that first day eight years ago. She'd very firmly told him that she had zero desire to be in his bed. And also, she was a damn good assistant. Better than even he could have predicted. He'd seen it in her eyes that first day. That hungry, desperate determination to succeed had been vibrating through her. Over the years, she'd proven herself over and over again. He would never diminish her success by suggesting anything other than a professional relationship.

Although, he'd been playing with an idea for the past year. Something that would make her more of an equal than a subordinate. And the more he thought about it, the more he thought the idea had merit.

And because he'd usually gone with his instincts and been proven right over and over again, he made the decision at that moment. The fact that she remembered one of his predictions from six months ago only confirmed how involved she was with the success of every aspect of his company.

"By the way, I'm making you a partner in the firm," he announced, then watched for her reaction.

Josh wasn't disappointed. Sloane's gorgeous blue eyes stared at him, the reddish-orange sauce dripping from the momentarily forgotten battered shrimp held aloft with her chopsticks.

"I'm sorry?" she blurted out finally.

He shrugged. "I'm making you a partner. You've been with me from the beginning and have done an excellent job here. You're an integral part of the company and a large reason for the success. So, I'm making you a partner."

With that, he turned back to his computer. "We need to shift some of these stocks in the Montegro Fund. It's not performing well enough yet."

Sloane continued to stare at Josh, not sure that she'd heard him correctly. A partner? He was making her a partner? What did that even mean?

But since he started throwing instructions to her, she needed to focus on those and figure out the meaning to his other comment later.

A half hour later, he sighed and stretched his arms over his head wearily. "Okay, that's enough for today," he said, leaning back against the sofa. "You look exhausted. Why don't you go out and sit by the pool with your sisters for a while?" Josh stood up and began gathering up the papers.

It was almost dinner time, but she was reluctant to leave him, knowing that he'd keep working if she left. "I'm fine," she replied, not wanting him to think she couldn't keep up with his schedule.

"Why don't you date?" he asked softly.

When Sloane turned, she found him leaning a shoulder against the wall. He looked amazingly virile in khaki slacks and a loose shirt, the muscles of his forearms drawing her gaze. She noticed the tanned column of his neck and his broad shoulders, his lean waist, and...well, all of him. Every time he did this, she couldn't seem to keep her eyes from surveying him.

And yeah, she knew he was muscular. Not because she'd ever been privileged to touch him. No way! But because she'd felt that strength last night in the casino, plus she'd seen him in workout clothes and after a long run. Many times actually. They traveled together, always shared a suite, and she knew the man. She'd even seen him swimming several times. He was...extraordinary!

"Sloane?" he prompted softly.

Was his voice huskier than a moment ago? She looked up at his face and noticed the intensity in those emerald eyes of his.

She cleared her throat, pushing the thoughts aside. She turned away and focused on packing up her bag. "I think that you date enough for both of us," she teased.

There was silence behind her and she turned, hoping that he hadn't taken offense. "I mean..."

"I know what you meant. But I don't date *that* much," he said. He smiled briefly. "Okay, so I used to. But recently..." he trailed off and shrugged. "So why don't you? There were several men admiring you last night in the casino, but you didn't even notice them."

She shrugged. "No one bothers to ask me out," she laughed.

"I don't believe that. You could have had any man in the casino last night, but you were oblivious to the attention."

Sloane sighed, leaning against the back of one of the hotel chairs. The truth was, she'd been too aware of Josh last night to notice anyone else. The way he'd touched her had felt...different.

Unfortunately, Josh was in one of his moods where he'd discovered a mystery and was determined to ferret it out. When Josh Starke discovered a puzzle, he was merciless until he figured it out.

She could offer him nothing more than complete honesty. Well, not complete. He didn't need to know about her interest in him, but she could explain why she didn't date other men. At least, she could tell him enough to satisfy his curiosity...she hoped.

"Well, there's the fact that my father vanished as soon as my mother informed him that she was pregnant." She laughed harshly, crossing her arms protectively over her chest. "Apparently, my father thought that my mother was enchanting enough for a roll in the hay, but when it came to anything more, he wasn't interested."

"That's...!"

She interrupted him, not wanting pity. "It's fine. I'm sure a therapist would tell me that I have abandonment issues. But since Rayne's biological father, and Pepper's too, did the same thing, I prefer to say that I have a healthy distrust for the romantic inclinations of men."

He waited, watching her carefully. "And?"

"And what?" she shrugged self-consciously. Damn the man for being so spookily perceptive.

"And what are the other reasons?"

She rubbed her forehead. "Well, there's also the issue of freakish levels of fertility among the women in my family. And men aren't interested in dating someone who refuses to have sex."

"You don't have sex?" he demanded, more than slightly stunned.

"Well, I've...um..." she blushed, wishing that the overhead lights weren't so bright. "No. I've never trusted a man enough to get to that point. Again, refer to issue A."

He stared for a moment, then nodded. "Abandonment issues and freakish fertility. What else?"

"Do I need more issues?" She asked, refusing to tell him that she'd never found any man that was more fascinating than he was. Boy, that would be a career killer, wouldn't it?!

"Probably not," he replied, still watching her with a strange look in his eyes. "But even if you don't want a long term commitment, why not dabble a bit? Why not try casual dating?"

"Like you do?" she replied, trying to tease him and lighten the mood. He was too intense at the moment, and it worried her for some reason. Why did she always want to make him feel better? He was so intense most of the time and it felt as if the sun came out whenever he smiled or relaxed. It gave her a triumphant feeling. Why, she didn't know. It had sort of evolved over the years.

Of course, when he sounded all grumpy and angry, she didn't bother him, preferring to keep her distance.

Odd, how their relationship had evolved over the past eight years together.

"What are you thinking about?" he asked, jerking her back to the present.

She stiffened, startled by what she had been contemplating. "Oh, um... well, just...?" she didn't have an explanation for what she'd been thinking.

"Can't come up with a good lie fast enough?" he teased, but she saw the truth in his eyes and sighed.

"No. I was thinking about how you're grumpy sometimes and...well, I just...?" she wasn't sure how to finish the sentence. No way would she admit that she enjoyed teasing him out of his bad moods, making him smile or, when he was being overly grumpy, silently demanding that he be more polite.

"And you tease me until I get so annoyed that I threaten to fire you?"

She laughed. "You've never threatened that, Josh," she said and stood up. "I'm going out to the pool. Will you join us? Or are you going to stay inside and work some more?"

Josh hesitated and Sloane wondered what he was thinking about. "You go ahead. I have some phone calls to make."

"I'll stay," she replied, moving back to the couch.

"No, there's nothing you can do to help. Go outside and enjoy the sunshine. We'll hit the casino again tonight, do a bit more sight-seeing tomorrow and see how we all feel about flying home after that."

She hesitated again, and he lifted one of those darkly sardonic eyebrows again. "Fine!" she grumbled. "I'll leave you to your hermit-like existence and go outside to revel in the sunshine, thinking about you holed up in the dark hotel suite making another billion dollars."

With that, she turned on her heel and walked out of the room, smiling at his laughter which followed her out.

Chapter 10

Josh watched Sloane as she walked gracefully along the edge of the pool towards her sisters, the revelations of earlier today hitting him hard. No one. No other man had *ever* touched her! It wasn't so much that he wanted to be her first, it was more that he wanted to be her last. The thought of being her first lover hadn't even occurred to him, but now...knowing that no other man had made love to her humbled him.

Those soft blushes had startled him. Plus the way she'd leaned into him over and over, the long looks, the intensity that was thick in the air whenever they were alone...or when they blocked out the world... all of it added up to interest. Intense interest, he realized. Apparently, he wasn't alone in his desire for something more than just a working relationship.

Not that they were merely co-workers. He considered her a friend and loved teasing her. She was a bit of a control freak and, although he understood her control issues, he still loved to tease her about them. She also loved herbal tea, refused to purchase anything at a clothing or shoe store unless it had been marked down several times, ate healthy foods until she couldn't stand them any longer and then binged on something unhealthy, loved M&Ms and ate them one color at a time, then move on to the next color – and the browns were always the first to go. Oh, and she loved her sisters intensely.

And that was just the superficial stuff. He knew that she loved taking care of people, but didn't let anyone abuse her. Some of the employees he'd hired over the past eight years had tried to take advantage of her generous heart and she'd easily put them in their place. Josh had gotten rid of those people pretty quickly, not wanting abusive personalities in his company, no matter how much profit they brought in.

Josh also knew that she was concerned about Jefferson and Wilma, treating them like her grandparents and visiting them whenever she could. She ran errands for Wilma, played chess with Jefferson, teased the old man about his drinking, and helped Wilma with the dishes whenever she ate at the main house.

As he contemplated her finer qualities, Josh watched as she lifted the sundress up and over her head, revealing a two piece bathing suit. Her figure was stunning! She was slender, but what she had was...perfect! Small breasts, tiny waist, and legs that seemed to go on forever. As he watched her spread the towel out over the lounge chair beside her sisters, Josh was dazed by her curves, his hands tightening on the concrete bannister of his balcony. His eyes burned and he realized that he hadn't blinked in too long. Rubbing his eyes, he groaned at the ache just looking at her produced.

Turning away, he walked back into the suite...but couldn't get the image of Sloane's perfect, slender curves out of his mind.

Chapter 11

"This is...amazing!" Pepper whispered, her eyes wide as she took in all of the glamour of the casino. "It's just...!" she paused and looked around. "I think I was too overwhelmed last night to really appreciate everything. But after lazing around by the pool all afternoon, I'm fully capable of recognizing the beauty of this room."

Sloane reached over and hugged Pepper, then glanced over her shoulder at Josh, who watched them with his usual brotherly amusement.

As usual, Rayne was silent as she took everything in, standing still... well, "still" relative to Pepper who was practically vibrating with excitement. Rayne wasn't bouncing, but anyone watching her would still see the excitement underneath her outwardly calm demeanor.

Rayne and Pepper couldn't hide their excitement and Sloane couldn't hide her happiness because her sisters were so excited at being here. She again looked for Josh. When he caught her eye, Sloane was startled at the blush that stole up her neck. A blush? How childish! And yet, she couldn't seem to stop the red flush from stealing higher along her cheeks.

Looking away, she shifted on her feet, feeling foolish for letting him see how much he affected her. She was his boss! Sloane cursed herself for being so ridiculously foolish whenever he looked at her like that. Or when he did extravagant things such as taking her sisters to a fabulously beautiful country. He was...impossible!

"Sir," a tuxedoed servant stepped up to Josh with a wooden box, which he opened with an elaborate flourish, revealing gambling chips.

"What's going on?" Sloane asked, staring at the box of gambling chips. There were significantly more chips than what he'd played with last night.

"These are for you ladies," Josh said as he took ten chips out of the box, handing them to Pepper, and doing the same for Rayne before trying to hand ten chips to Sloane, who pulled back.

"You're giving us chips again?" Pepper asked, staring at the gambling chips in her hand with a stunned, wary expression.

"Yes. Go have fun and enjoy yourselves," he told Pepper and Rayne.

They both stared back down at their hands filled with the square, heavy chips, then up at Josh. "How much are these worth?" Pepper dared to ask.

"They are one dollar chips," he told them.

Pepper and Rayne visibly relaxed, their smiles brightening. "Cool! Ten dollars!"

They wandered off, diving into the crowds of beautifully dressed people, completely unaware of Sloane's open-mouthed stare at Josh. But before she could stop them, Rayne and Pepper were gone, happily off to gamble with their "one dollar" chips.

"You lied!" Sloane gasped and turned to glare at Josh. Even the casino employee was a bit astonished, but he hid his reaction better, simply turning with a straight face and walking away, having done his job and probably heading into the servants area to announce the stunning lie one of their patrons told to the ladies in his group.

"What did I lie about?" Josh asked, chuckling at her outraged expression as he took her arm and pulled her to his side, out of the way of others on the main pathway from the casino and bar.

"This casino doesn't *have* one dollar chips!" she hissed under her breath. To be honest, she felt a bit breathless with the way his hand lingered on her arm, sliding higher, then lower as he maneuvered them out of the way. It was all a repeat of last night and she was both excited and nervous about how close she wanted to get to him.

"Really?" he asked, lifting her hand and placing several chips in it. "How very silly of me."

Sloane tried to push the chips back into his hand, but he wouldn't let her. "You're never silly, Josh! How much are those chips *really* worth?"

"It doesn't matter. Just let them have fun. And you should do the same, Sloane," he told her, putting a hand to the small of her back. "Just relax and enjoy the night."

He stopped a passing waiter. "Champagne for the ladies and a whiskey for me." The waiter nodded and turned, eagerly moving to obey Josh's order.

Sloane glared up at Josh, not even going to ask how the waiter would know to bring champagne to Pepper and Rayne. A long time ago, she'd stopped trying to figure out how staff at these high end establishments knew things. They just knew.

"How much are these chips really worth?" she repeated.

He guided her over to the roulette table again. "Why don't you find out?" he suggested as he placed a chip on one of the numbers. "I won with you by my side last night. Perhaps you'll win with me beside you. We'll have to discover who is the better risk taker."

The roulette ball bounced around. The roulette guy, Sloane wasn't sure what he was called but he looked very stern as the ball bounced, the wheel spun, and everyone placed bets on the numbers on the felt table.

She watched Josh place the chip on a white number and almost choked on her gasp. "Wait! What are you doing?" she gasped.

"All bets final," the man called, just when Sloane would have grabbed that dang chip right off of the table.

"What have you done?" she sighed, turning away, unable to watch.

"You need to just enjoy the excitement, Sloane," Josh told her, his lips dangerously close to her ear. She jumped slightly, startled by his proximity. There were a lot of people around, but...could he know? Could he see how the subtle brush of his lips against the shell of her ear caused her to...?

Shiver.

Yes! He caught her reaction! And then...when she glanced up at him, Sloane watched his eyes dilate so that there was almost no green left, his eyes dark with...desire?

"Vingt Huit!" the guy announced.

"You won," his lips whispered, huskily. She'd heard that grumbling sound several times over the past eight years and had always assumed it meant Josh was in a bad mood. But he didn't look grumpy now. What did it mean?

"I won what?" she asked, her gaze dropping to his lips, wondering what it would feel like if he kissed her. Dangerous, pointless thought but...she couldn't stop wondering about it.

"About ten thousand dollars," he replied.

Sloane blinked. "Excuse me?" she demanded, and turned to look down at the table. Sure enough, where her single chip had previously rested, there was a stack of those square chips! "What?" she gasped, looking around? But the ball was spinning again. How long had she stood there staring up at Josh? Had anyone else noticed?

She started to reach out to pull those chips away, not wanting to lose any of Josh's money.

He took her hand in his, pulling her hand back. "You can't pull the bet now, Sloane. You'll have to let it ride."

The ball bounced and clanked, slowing and Sloane almost expired from lack of oxygen as she waited tensely for the ball to finally stop.

"Trente et un!" the man called out, and with a swoop of an L shaped-like cane, he pulled all of the chips away.

"Wait!" she cried, then stopped when she heard Josh's bark of laughter. "But I didn't mean to bet anything!"

"You win and lose," he told her. He handed her another chip. "Here, choose another number."

"No!" she gasped, curling her fingers around the chip, holding it close to her breast. "I won't do it."

He grinned when she frowned up at him, daring him. And of course, this was Josh, and he always dared. He placed another chip on the number twenty-six. "There. Your age. That should be good luck."

She shook her head and backed up a step, right into his hard chest. His hands moved to her hips, resting heavily on her body and she shivered again. Sloane looked up at him over her shoulder, about to move away but his hands tightened, not allowing her to move even an inch.

"Stay where you are," he ordered in that grumpy voice again.

"Why?" she whispered, then he shifted and she knew! She felt his body's reaction and her mouth fell open, shocked that she could...that he would...!

"Vingt-six!" the man announced, startling them. All the other chips were whisked away, but Sloane's chip remained. A moment later, twenty more chips were added to it.

"Good grief!" she gasped and pulled the chips closer, having learned her lesson on the last bet and not waiting for that speedy man to fling that metal ball once again.

"I'm not betting again," she told him firmly.

"Fine," he replied easily. Sloane might have sighed with relief, but she knew that look. It was a dangerous look. One that foretold he was going to get her to do something she wasn't going to like.

Sure enough, he led her away from the roulette table and over to another table. "Have a seat."

Sloane sat down, feeling a huge amount of relief. Sitting meant she was free from gambling, right?

Nope!

"Chips please," he said to the dealer.

Immediately, the dealer pulled ten of the red chips out of her box and handed them to her, then slid an electronic tablet towards him. Josh signed the receipt as if he were buying a pack of gum!

"It's blackjack. I know that you know how to play this because we've played it on the plane."

Sloane nodded, feeling a little better. At least with blackjack, there was a touch of skill to it.

And yet, fifteen minutes later, all of her chips were gone while there was a huge stack of chips sitting in front of Josh.

"Here," he gave her another ten chips.

"No!" She shook her head. "I'm not gambling anymore."

Josh nodded to the dealer. Since they were the only two people at this table, there was a bit more leeway. If the table were full, the dealer would be stricter about the pace of play, the other gamblers demanding a faster pace.

He didn't let her quit. She won some hands and lost others, but Josh won consistently, his stack increasing steadily while her stack remained pretty much the same. But at least she didn't lose any money.

Every time she checked her fluted glass, it seemed to be full, no matter how much she drank. But after a few hours, she didn't want any more. And even more surprising, she *was* actually having a good time! Josh teased her whenever she pulled back on a hand, trying to coax her into being more adventurous. But she remained cautious with his money, shaking her head as he continued to win.

"How do you do that?" she asked when the dealer slid over another large stack of chips. She had no idea how much money was in front of him now, but she suspected that it was well over her annual salary.

There was a crowd cheering in one corner and Sloane looked over at the table. "Oh no!" she gasped, seeing Rayne and Pepper in the crowd. But upon closer inspection, Sloane realized that they weren't in the crowd, the crowd seemed to be surrounding her sisters!

"What's going on?" Sloane asked Josh, missing the look of heat that flared back to life in his green eyes when she touched his arm.

"I don't know. Let's go find out," he said and lifted his hand. Immediately, a servant appeared with one of those wooden boxes, but this time, it was empty.

"Cashing out," he said to the man, who bowed...actually bowed!

He handed over Sloane's chips too. "Ms. Abbot is cashing in as well."

She shook her head. "I'm not cashing in anything. Those aren't my chips, they are yours."

Josh ignored her, nodding to the servant who immediately moved away with all of their winnings.

"You won them," he argued, putting that hot hand to the small of her back again.

"Umm...not really," she whispered, wondering if he were burning a hole in the simple, black dress she was wearing. His hand...she could feel each of his fingers and the slight pressure that he applied in order to tell her which way to go. And because it was Josh, she followed his silent instructions until they reached the table in question.

It was craps, she realized. This was one of the more complicated games, in her opinion. There was no skill. Just pure luck.

The crowd seemed to magically part when Josh stepped closer. Sloane almost snickered at the quick respect he garnered, but that hand smoothed up her back. In warning? She looked up at him and saw that he watching Rayne and Pepper.

"Do it again, Pepper!" Rayne exclaimed, her cheeks bright with excitement.

Pepper bounced, of course, and blew on the dice, then tossed them down the craps table. There was a long moment of breathlessness as everyone waited, watching the dice as they tumbled to a halt against the back wall of the table. Then there was a huge roar of applause and surprise when the dice turned up as sixes.

"Was that good?" Sloane whispered to Josh.

He leaned down and murmured, "They've just doubled their money as well as everyone else's."

Pepper was jumping up and down, completely unconcerned with her lack of sophistication. Even Rayne was almost bouncing. Both were grinning from ear to ear and looked a bit dazed.

"Again?" Pepper asked, glancing at Rayne.

Rayne bit her lower lip, then laughed, both of them shaking their heads. "No. We've probably won about a hundred dollars now, so let's quit while we're ahead."

Both of them scooped up their winnings and laughed as the rest of the crowd tried to get them to change their mind. "You can't stop when you're on a streak," one man protested.

Pepper and Rayne simply smiled, beguiling the men and causing the women to gnash their teeth in jealousy.

The staff member with the odd looking box returned, looking expectantly at Rayne and Pepper.

Josh stepped forward, explaining. "If you give this man your chips, he will cash them in for you. He'll have a cashier's check waiting for you when you're ready to leave."

Rayne's eyes widened. "Oh, um...well, can't we just get cash? I mean, it's just...it's only about a hundred dollars, right?"

Sloane carefully watched the casino employee's reaction. His lips quirked upwards at the corners ever so slightly. Bingo!

"You are a horrible man!" she hissed, emphasizing each word.

"You wound me with your harsh words, my dear," he replied, but the glint in those devilish eyes told her more than his words. He didn't give her a chance to argue. He turned to the box-man with a curt nod. Immediately, Pepper and Rayne dumped their chips into the box.

"But how will we know how much we won?" Pepper asked, her eyes following the box as the man closed the lid and left.

"You each won just over one hundred thousand dollars," he explained. "Sloane won about twenty thousand because she didn't get as into the spirit of the evening as you two did." He put a hand on Sloane's back, nudging her forward slightly. "I think it is time to adjourn to the bar for a drink. Shall we?"

He started moving, but the sisters simply stood there, looking stunned.

"Come along, ladies," he urged.

Finally, he got them moving towards the hotel bar and seated in a corner booth. He ordered waters all around, and leaned back against the luxurious upholstery, watching them with intense satisfaction, all of them silent for once as the shock of his announcement hit each of them.

Pepper was the first to snap out of her stupor. "Why didn't you tell us?" she asked, her lips apparently numb with shock.

"I didn't tell you because then you wouldn't have had any fun. All three of you have earned your degrees. I wanted you to have fun to-night."

Rayne shivered, her arms tightly crossed over her stomach. "What if we'd lost?"

"Then you still would have had a fun evening and you never would have been the wiser."

Pepper opened her mouth, then snapped it shut. She looked at Rayne, then at Sloane, who was trembling slightly, still shocked at the amount of money that had been gambled over the past several hours. Pepper's eyes narrowed.

"Wait. You just said all *three* of us graduated."

Rayne looked at Pepper, then at Sloane, who looked up, surprised. Then all three of them turned to look at Josh.

"Yes, Sloane earned her business degree as well," he announced.

Again, there was a long moment of stunned silence, then Pepper and Rayne screamed...and pounced on their oldest sister. The elegant atmosphere and sophistication of this corner of the bar was obliterated with the noise of the two youngest laughing and crying as they hugged Sloane, demanding answers one on top of the other.

"Why didn't you tell us?" Rayne demanded.

"Because I wanted the focus to be on you two. This is *your* special weekend," she told them.

Rayne snorted in disgust and Pepper rolled her eyes. "I can't believe you've been going to school all this time and didn't tell us! How could you be so sneaky?"

She laughed. "I wasn't trying to be sneaky," she admitted. "But we've all been working pretty hard, studying and going to classes. So both of you have been gone quite a bit lately. There were many nights that I'd be studying at the kitchen table, but you were both at your respective libraries until late so you never saw me."

Again, Sloane missed the expression in Josh's eyes, but Rayne didn't. She caught it and wondered about it, and decided she'd pull Sloane to the side and ask about it later.

Out of the corner of her eye, Rayne caught sight of a man who was taller and...seemed more dangerous than the other patrons in the exclusive bar. And he was watching them.

Having dealt with other men's intrusiveness over the years, she stared right back at him, daring him to invade their privacy even with his eyes. But he didn't react like most would have. He didn't look away in embarrassment. In fact, just the opposite. He locked eyes with her, almost as if he were trying to tell her something. When he lifted his dark eyebrow in question or...challenge? She wasn't sure what he was attempting to convey, but she felt her heart begin to pound.

Turning away, she focused on her sisters, not sure if she was angry that her sister had accomplished something so wonderful while working a more than full time job, embarrassed that they'd been so self-absorbed that she and Pepper had gone on their merry way, earning their own degrees while it had taken her older sister seven years to finish hers, or intense pride that her sister had done something almost miraculous.

But the whole time she smiled and listened as Pepper questioned Sloane, Rayne was painfully aware of that man. He didn't move and he didn't even try to hide his curiosity. How rude! How arrogant! What a jerk, she thought.

Chapter 12

Sloane fought the urge to curl up in her leather chair and fall asleep. The low hum of the plane's engines had always been the perfect background noise for her, luring her into a deep, dreamless sleep as they traveled across the globe.

But something was wrong. Rayne was sitting stiffly in her chair, staring blankly out the nearest window. Since the jet was flying above the thick clouds, Sloane knew that Rayne wasn't looking at anything specific.

"Hey," she said softly. When Rayne turned her head, Sloane saw the pain there and immediately jumped up from her chair. Taking the seat next to Rayne, Sloane took her sister's hand. "What's wrong?"

Rayne forced her lips to smile. "I'm just...nervous about leaving you and Pepper when I head to California," she said. "It will be the first time that the three of us will be apart."

Sloane watched Rayne's eyes and knew that her sister was lying. Well, mostly lying, she mentally amended. But why? What had happened that was bothering her so deeply? "Honey, you know that you can talk to me about *anything*, right?"

For a long moment, Rayne fought back the threatening tears and Sloane held her breath, wondering if Rayne would tell her what was wrong. But her sister's strength won out and the tears abated. Rayne smiled and covered their clasped hands with her free hand. "I'm fine," she whispered. "Sad about leaving. That's all it is. I promise."

Sloane didn't believe her and, when she glanced over at Pepper, she suspected that their youngest sister didn't agree either. "Fine," she said to Rayne. "You're not ready to talk, but know that I'm here for you, okay? No matter what's going on, you can talk to me."

Rayne's chin trembled and she laid her head on Sloane's shoulder.

"Thanks!" But she remained silent. Whatever demons were troubling her, Rayne wasn't ready to talk about them. Not just yet.

Sloane didn't move, but her thoughts were going about a hundred miles an hour. What had happened over the past few days? Had someone said something to her over the long weekend? Had she lost the money she'd won? Instinctively, Sloane knew that it wasn't just about traveling to another state. That might be part of it, but the three of them had talked and cried about their departures already.

No, something else was bothering her serious, strong sister. Sloane knew that she'd just have to wait it out. Rayne would talk when she'd mentally worked through the issue.

Chapter 13

"Okay, so tell Charlie to shift the funds towards the Annex issue and change the weighting," Josh snapped.

Sloane smiled, writing down his instructions with efficient accuracy. Josh's mind was constantly working, always sifting through the data that he knew and searching for more so that he could make an informed decision on where to move his clients' money so it earned the best results. Over the years, Sloane had learned to interpret his generally curt instructions into more actionable directions.

"Are you laughing at me again?" he asked.

Sloane glanced up from her laptop, still smiling. "Yes," she replied honestly. They'd been working in his penthouse today, needing to focus away from the office.

Josh leaned back against the soft suede of his sofa, clasping his hands behind his head. "Care to share the joke?"

"Nope," she replied, closing her laptop and stuffing it into her bag. "Anything else?"

"Yes," he told her and stood up. "Dinner." Josh walked towards the kitchen as Sloane's heart started pounding. Just watching him was doing strange things to her now. What had changed? Why couldn't she just see Josh as her boss?

"Um...Josh, I need to..."

He didn't bother to turn around when he interrupted her. "You need to come into the kitchen and talk to me while I cook dinner. You're not going home to the empty cottage again."

She stiffened, but he simply disappeared into the kitchen. "I'm fine," she muttered to her lap, then sniffed softly.

"You're not fine," he countered.

Her head snapped up, seeing him standing in the open space between

the great room and the kitchen, startled and more than slightly discon-
certed. "I thought you were in the kitchen already," she grumbled.

"I know. Come on, Sloane. I know that you skipped lunch and you're
in such a foul mood that you're going to go home to a dark cottage and
not cook anything for dinner. So, you're not leaving here until you eat
something."

And with those words, he disappeared into the kitchen.

For a long moment, Sloane just stood there by the matching suede
sofas, glaring at the wide doorway between the living room and the
kitchen. But in the end, she acknowledged that she was hungry. Starving, actually. And he was right, she didn't want to go home to that dark
house and be alone again.

But it was dangerous to stay here. Without her sisters' chaos surrounding her, Sloane had too much time on her hands. Every night,
she was alone with her own thoughts and every night, those thoughts
turned to Josh. Without her sisters around to distract her, Sloane
wasn't able to hide her feelings. Not even from herself.

Plus, after their time in Monaco, there had been an extra level of tension between them. A tension that, if she was right, was pulling them
down a dangerous path.

"Sloane!" he bellowed.

Sloane jumped and glared in his general direction. Unfortunately, the
wall separating them didn't allow him to see her glare. So instead, she
walked towards the kitchen and stepped into the bright lights.

"What?"

"Come help me," he ordered, waving the knife towards the peppers
and onions on a separate cutting board. He was busy slicing up the
chicken into thin pieces and he obviously wanted her to do the same
with the red, yellow, and green peppers.

"You could have just asked," she grumbled, walking over to the countertop and picking up the knife.

"I could have, but it wouldn't have gotten you in here," he countered.
"Talk to me. What's going on in your head?"

Sloane sighed and started slicing the red pepper into thin strips. "I
just...I miss my sisters," she told him, which was only half the truth.
"We call each other almost every day, but it isn't the same."

"Are they doing okay? Their new jobs going well?"

She sliced and he sliced and Sloane relaxed. They'd cooked together
hundreds of times over the years and this felt...good. Normal! Yes, it
was a normal scene that they'd replayed over and over again. Josh
liked to cook and she hated it. So they'd sort of developed a routine.
Whenever she came to his place, which had changed over the past eight

years, they'd work for several hours and then he'd cook dinner for them. They'd usually work for another few hours after dinner and then she'd head home to her sisters.

But tonight, there wasn't any need to hurry home.

For some reason, that felt significant, although Sloane wasn't willing to consider why.

"Tell me what they are up to," he encouraged and put a wok on the stove, heating up the oil.

For the next twenty minutes, they talked about Rayne and Pepper, Wilma and Jefferson, and a few of the others in the company while Josh cooked. Sloane selected a bottle of wine and opened it, pouring each of them a glass, and perched on one of the counter stools.

It was just a normal evening. They'd done this hundreds of times, she told herself.

So, why did it feel so different?

They ate the delicious stir fry at the counter, the conversation never lagging, but by the end of the meal, when Sloane picked up their plates to rinse them and slide them into the dishwasher, Josh walked over to stand behind her. "Sloane, what's *really* wrong?" he asked softly, his voice deep and husky. The sound sent shivers down over her body and she straightened stiffly, her back to him, as she fought her body's reaction to that tone.

Closing her eyes, she braced her hands against the sink. "It's different," she murmured.

She felt him move closer. Felt his body heat warm her back.

"What's different?" he asked, his voice huskier.

"This," she whispered back, bowing her head in defeat. "Something changed in Monaco and now, everything feels different."

He sighed and she felt his warm breath brush against her neck.

"Sloane." He said her name as if it were a caress. Then she felt his strong hand on her back and lifted her head. Slowly, feeling as if she were dreaming again, she turned around. He was closer than she'd thought, but it wasn't bad. In fact, she wanted him...closer.

"I feel it too," he admitted. "But I don't think that it's only been since Monaco." He put a hand on either side of her waist and...shifted so that there was barely an inch of space separating their bodies. "It's been happening for a while now, hasn't it?"

She held her breath for a long moment, staring at his chest. But Sloane hated cowardice, so she lifted her eyes to look at his face. "Yes," she whispered in reply.

"Maybe it's time we did something about it."

She trembled and his hands tightened on her waist. "I don't want to lose our friendship, Josh. You mean so much to me."

Slowly, he leaned his head down and kissed the top of her head. "We won't lose our friendship, Sloane. I won't let that happen." Then he kissed her cheek.

His lips were warm and soft and she closed her eyes, savoring the soft caresses, but wanting more. Turning her head slightly, ever so slightly, she blinked and...he kissed her lips. It was just a brief touch...too brief.

When had her hands moved to his shoulders? Before she could re-member, he kissed her again, his lips brushing back and forth, coaxing her to participate. Sloane was all for participation, but she didn't want brief, teasing kisses. This was Josh and she couldn't count how many erotic dreams she'd had about this man. It was sort of a habit now, to fall asleep and dream about him making love to her.

So instead of accepting the brief kisses, she lifted up onto her toes and, completely out of character, deepened the kiss. For a brief mo-ment, Josh allowed her control. But that was it, just that moment. With strong hands, he pulled her against his hard chest and took control, nibbling her lower lip until she opened her mouth for him. That's when she lost both control and sense of time. Her hands slid up his shoulders into his hair, her fingers tangling in those dark locks, then holding him in place when she thought he was going to pull away.

He didn't. His mouth just moved from her lips to her neck, teasing the too-sensitive skin there. She gasped, pressing her body against his as she tilted her head back, giving him better access. Her hands tightened in his hair and she gasped when he found an extra sensitive spot just under her ear.

Suddenly, she felt his hands against her bare skin. She moaned with delight as his hands traced along the bare skin of her back, her waist. She trembled as his mouth moved back to hers and she felt frantic, needing to kiss him more and deeper, wanting to feel his hands on more of her skin. She was desperate, terrified that he might stop. Mindlessly, she shifted against him, unconsciously trying to absorb every touch, every sensation before he called a stop to this madness.

Josh couldn't believe how good Sloane felt! She was almost as wild for him as he was for her and he couldn't get enough of her. He hadn't meant for things to go this far. He'd meant only to kiss her, to test the waters and see if she would pull away. But her hands were in his hair, touching his skin, and her touch drove him wild!

He scooped her up and placed her on the countertop. This brought her higher so that their heads were almost aligned. She was such a small thing, but every inch of her felt good against his throbbing body. He needed more, needed to...

Her blouse came up and over her head and he wasn't sure how he'd gotten the buttons undone. "Sloane," he growled, seeing her soft breasts encased in the delicate lace of her bra. It wasn't the fanciest lingerie he'd ever seen, but somehow it was the prettiest.

And then it was gone! He deftly unclasped the bra and tossed it away. "You're more beautiful than I imagined," he groaned, leaning down to take a nipple into his mouth. Her hiss made him want to howl, but the lure of her nipple, the aching need to feel that taut peak in his mouth taunted him. He felt her legs wrap around his waist and he lost control. Lifting her up into his arms, he kissed her again while carrying her to his bedroom. With her arms around his neck and her legs around his waist, he couldn't think properly. He'd fantasized about this too many times and the reality was so much more intense!

Kicking the door to his bedroom closed, he laid her on the bed. For a long moment, he continued to kiss her, feeling her body shift against his and it was all he could do to pull back long enough to ask, "Are you sure about this?"

Sloane looked up into his eyes, the green was almost luminescent in the soft light. "Yes!" she whispered back, her fingers still in his hair. He couldn't hold back after that one word. It was all the permission he needed and his mouth moved back to hers. Kissing her for a long time, he reveled in this moment, enjoying the sensations of finally having Sloane in his arms, in his bed!

That's when he felt her soft hands against the bare skin of his neck and it wasn't enough. Pulling away, he ripped his shirt open, scattering buttons across the floor, and reached for her, placing her hands on his bare chest. "Touch me, Sloane!" he groaned, then moved back to her neck, exploring every inch of her skin and finding more places that made her tremble and gasp. But his favorite place was her breasts. She was so slender and her breasts were barely a handful. Just perfect, he thought and kissed the peaks, taking them into his mouth and sucking, teasing, nibbling gently until he knew what she liked the best. He moved to the other breast and enjoyed her reactions from his ministrations there too.

He needed more. His hands moved to the zipper on the side of her skirt and tugged it down, then pushed her skirt off, down over her legs. He should probably drape her wool skirt over a chair or something because he knew that she took extremely good care of her clothes, but he could barely breathe, much less care for her clothes. She was naked except for a prim pair of white, cotton panties. And beautiful!

He tried to pull those tantalizing panties down, but in his urgency, he ripped them off instead. Then she was naked. Completely naked and all his!

As gently as possible, aware that she'd never done this before, he moved his fingers down her stomach, caressing her inner thighs, wanting to show her what it could be like.

She gasped, her legs moving wider, and the sight of her left him breathless.

Pushing away, he stood beside the bed, stripped off the remainder of his clothes, and grabbed a condom from the bedside table.

She lifted up onto her elbows, those fascinating blue eyes of hers watching him. But his undoing was her tongue wetting her lips as he rolled the condom down his shaft. "Damn it, Sloane!" he growled. That look, her tongue, and her slender, amazing body was too powerful of an enticement. He moved back to her but...instead of pressing his shaft into her body as he wanted to, he pressed her legs wider and, with a peek at her pink folds, moved down.

"Josh, I don't...!"

"Just a taste, Sloane," he assured her, lying through his teeth. He wanted more than a taste. He wanted all of her! He wanted to slam into her and feel her muscles clench around him, but he wanted to feel her climax, feel her hands clench in his hair as she pressed against his mouth.

With that intent in mind, he teased those glistening folds, his shoulders pushing her legs wider. He watched with fascination as he slid one of his fingers into her heat, making her back arch. When his tongue flicked against that nub, he almost laughed at the moan she made. She was so damned responsive! Every touch of his tongue caused her to shiver and tremble against his mouth. Devouring her, he teased and touched and tasted until...he felt her climax with every one of his senses and it was a heady, erotic moment.

Moving over her, he took her hands in his, not to hold them away, but to feel her body's reaction more completely as he pressed slowly into her heat.

"You okay?" he asked, feeling on fire, trying to move slowly because he knew that she was a virgin, but...damn, she felt good! Too good!

"Oh Sloane!" he groaned, watching her face. He noticed her pretty white teeth biting her lower lip. "Am I hurting you?" he asked, pulling back.

Sloane's eyes whipped open and she pulled her hands away, her nails digging into his butt to stop his retreat. "Don't!" she gasped, then arched her back to take him deeper. "Please...don't stop!"

She felt as well as heard his rumbling laughter and smiled, lifting her legs higher and rolling her hips. "Just...yes, like that!"

He pressed into her deeper and deeper before pulling out and thrusting again. He felt so incredibly good! "Yes!" she whispered, turning her head slightly so she wouldn't reveal too much.

"Sloane, look at me," he ordered.

"I can't," she replied back, her voice a bit squeaky.

"I'm not moving again until you do."

She moaned at his demanding tone, but turned her head, looking right into his crystal green eyes. "Please," she shivered.

Slowly, he pressed fully into her. Sloane felt a small pop, but not the pain she'd been expecting. With a smile, she shifted again, allowing her body to adjust to his delicious invasion. "You feel so good," she told him, then bit her lip, startled that she'd said it out loud.

He laughed, and started moving, thrusting slowly into her heat. "As do you," he replied.

She laughed as well and was startled by it. Sloane had never thought that laughter would be a part of sex. It had been frantic right up until that moment but...okay, when he shifted like that, she felt that driving urgency again.

"Faster!" she sobbed, shifting her body, reaching for that blissful release. "Please, Josh!"

He shifted, moving his hands so that they were underneath her back slightly, holding her shoulders and then...he moved faster, shifting his hips so that every thrust brought her closer and closer.

Sloane held onto Josh, feeling every tingle building higher and higher and then... "Josh!" she screamed, this climax bigger and more intense than the last one. All she could do was hold onto his shoulders as he continued to thrust into her. With a groan of his own, his body tightened and his climax sent her over into yet another orgasm, clinging to him as the only solid object in her world.

A long time later, Sloane opened her eyes to find Josh staring down at her, his green eyes...victorious.

"What?" she whispered flexing her fingers and arms. They were stiff after that explosion and she...good grief, she was still clinging to him!

"Stop it," he growled, lowering his head to kiss her gently.

When he lifted his head again, she licked her lips, tasting his presence there. "Um...stop what?" she asked, not sure what the correct protocol was after having sex. Was she doing something wrong? Should she... just get up and leave? What was the polite thing to do in this situation?

"Stop second guessing yourself," he ordered softly, then kissed her again. He pulled out of her body and stood up. "Don't move. I'll be right back."

Josh walked towards what she assumed was a bathroom, and she curled up, pulling the soft comforter over her. Staring up at the ceiling, she bit her lip, trying to decide what to do. But at the moment, her body was tingling with so much...happiness...it was hard to get her mind to work properly. She wanted to laugh and dance. She wanted to tip toe towards that bathroom and watch him, see his body fully in the light.

And then the water shut off and the light flipped off. She heard as well as felt his footsteps coming back towards the bed and...trembled.

"You moved," he growled, coming onto the bed and bracing himself over her. "You look a bit stunned. Did I hurt you?" he asked, pulling the blankets away.

"No!" she smiled. "None of...that...was painful."

He peeled more of the blanket away so that he could pull her into his arms. He reached out and switched off the light, pulling the covers over both of them. "I'm glad."

She shifted against him, not understanding what was going on. "Shouldn't I head home?" she whispered, feeling strange. It felt good but...this was Josh! She shouldn't be here!

"Don't go home," he murmured, already sounding sleepy. "Stay here with me tonight."

Sloane didn't move, but she felt the muscles in his body slowly relax as he drifted off to sleep. Sloane tried to do the same, but she was just... too wound up.

Sex! She'd actually had sex with Josh! And it had been so much better than anything she'd dreamed about. Her fantasies were mere shadows of the reality! Every touch, every sigh, every thrust had been so much...more! Just everything about it had been more!

She wanted to snuggle up to him, but Sloane resisted the urge. Not because he'd notice, but because she'd notice. And she might actually fall asleep. But...she needed to leave. To head back to her house and shower. She felt sticky and strangely alive. She wanted to wake him up and convince him to do that all over again but...she looked at his profile in the shadows. He looked exhausted. Josh always pushed himself too hard, she thought as love filled her chest to the point of bursting.

No longer able to conceal her feelings, she let herself accept that she was completely, madly in love. She loved him so absolutely that her heart ached. It wasn't just sex, she told herself, although...she smiled, thinking about the way he'd touched her and the tender way he'd initiated her into the world of lovemaking.

Her feelings were definitely mixed with feelings of joy because of the sex, but she'd felt love for Josh before tonight. In fact, she'd probably been in love with him for years. When had her emotions shifted from hatred to friendship to love? She couldn't remember any specific moment, but as she'd gotten to know him over the years, she'd understood him better. He might be gruff and demanding, but he was more than fair and outrageously generous. But love...Sloane wasn't sure when that had happened either. She'd denied her love for him for so long, it had skewed her perceptions. Still, she loved him. Loved him with all of her heart.

She loved his strengths and weaknesses, loved all of his quirky habits, and she loved the way he took care of the people in his life. She loved... him. That's it. That's all of it. She loved him because of who he was, not because of what he represented.

And that love warmed her heart and...scared her to death! Sloane knew that he didn't love her back. No way. He wasn't that kind of a man. He was too focused on work and...well, that's what she'd do as well. Sloane knew that she loved him too much to burden him with her feelings.

With that in mind, she shifted again, looking up at his dark jawline and the ridiculously long lashes that lay against his skin. His hard muscles were...tempting, but he needed his rest.

Slipping slowly away so she didn't wake him, Sloane gathered up her clothes and tip toed out of the bedroom. Dressing outside, she realized that her underwear was completely ruined. With a smile, she tucked them into her purse and smoothed her skirt down over her hips, hoping that no one would notice she wasn't wearing panties! She smiled to herself as she grabbed her bag and slipped out the front door, setting the security alarm. She knew his codes since she'd been the one to have the system installed. She'd shown him how to reset the alarm, but he'd never changed the code.

A half hour later, she pulled into the space beside her cottage. Everything was dark inside and she stared at the small house. She'd lived here for eight years. Eight wonderful, challenging, scary years.

And she was in love with Josh Starke. Good grief, how the world had changed.

Stepping out of her car, she moved silently through the house, listening for sounds. But there weren't any because Pepper and Rayne were gone. Off to start their own lives.

Instead of thinking about her sisters, she showered and changed into a tee shirt, found another pair of panties, and slipped into bed. She was asleep within seconds.

Chapter 14

Sloane stepped into the office the next morning, her knees quivering with fear and embarrassment. She'd loved being with him last night, reveling in his arms and feeling the power of his touch. He kissed as if he'd been taught by a master and...the way he'd made her body sing? She hadn't thought that was possible!

The office was dark and quiet, thankfully. It allowed her to move down the hallway towards her own office and get settled in before she had to face the reality of what she'd done. Gone were the feelings of happiness she'd felt last night, replaced with anxiety over Josh's potential regret for what they'd done together.

With a sigh, she settled into her chair, connected her laptop and, surrounded by her familiar work world, felt balanced and in control again. Working here was good, she reminded herself. She loved her job and... well, she *respected* Josh. It wasn't love. Even after last night, she didn't love him. Not really. Her revelations last night had been...!

Closing her eyes, she sighed and bowed her head. She loved him. Loved him completely. He wasn't perfect. But he was pretty amazing. And she loved him so damn much that it hurt sometimes.

Like right now!

Blinking back the tears, she focused on her computer, needing to find the peace that usually came from her job. From controlling this small portion of her world. She loved her job and how she organized everyone in this office, took care of them, ensured that they had what that they needed. Especially Josh.

Would he fire her now that they'd...?

No, he wouldn't, but their relationship would change. It had to. They'd done...things. So many things with and to each other last night. Goodness, she felt her cheeks heat up at the memory!

"You left me!"

Sloane jerked backwards, startled.

Looking up at Josh, she was startled by how angry he appeared. Sloane couldn't remember another time when he'd looked so furious!

He moved silently over the plush carpeting until he stood on the other side of her desk. Then he leaned over, bracing his fists on her desk until he was less than a foot away from her face. "You left me, Sloane. And I'm *not* happy about it."

Sloane took in his angry, glittering eyes, and saw that muscle twitching along his jawline. Not good, she thought, unconsciously licking her lips.

"I just thought...that...well, that we would be more comfortable if we pretended that last night hadn't happened," she whispered, wishing that her voice sounded more confident. But with him this close, all she wanted to do was reach out and run a finger along his jaw. Maybe lean forward and kiss him, feel the power of his lips teasing hers. She wanted to press her body against his and feel that sensation of happiness when his arms wrapped around her body.

His eyes moved over her features, as if he were thinking the same things.

"Is that what you *really* want?"

She swallowed back the pain at the thought of never feeling his arms around her. "That's probably the best idea," she replied, hiding her hands under the desk so that he wouldn't see her fingers. They were trembling with the need to touch him.

"You're right, that's probably the best course of action," he agreed. Then his head slowly turned to the left and right. "Unfortunately, that's not what's going to happen between us, Sloane."

"It's not?" she croaked out.

"No." He straightened his tall, powerful body and came around to the other side of the desk. "We've ignored this sexual attraction for each other for too long," he explained in an almost conversational tone. "And it hasn't dissipated. Not for me at least." He took her hand, tugging her to her feet. "After last night," he pulled her closer and closer, leaning back against her desk and pulling her between his thighs, "I know that you feel the same way. We are going to explore this."

He didn't give her a chance to argue. He simply covered her lips with his and, after a fraction of a second when she tried to resist, she exploded with the need to kiss him back. It wasn't a conscious decision to let her hands slide up his perfectly tailored suit jacket and press herself against him until she could feel all of him against her softness. It was more like a growing need to touch and be touched that overwhelmed her and there was no decision to be made. It was just need and desire and desperate moans. The pins she'd carefully placed in her hair this morning were dislodged as his hand wove into her hair, pulling her head back so that he could deepen the kiss.

And then he stopped. Sloane looked up at him, startled that he would dare to stop! She whimpered and tightened her fingers on his hair.

"I knew it!" he growled, his hands tightening on her bottom as he lifted her against his erection. "I knew that this wasn't over! But damn it, Sloane, I was so furious when I woke up and you weren't there this morning!" He sighed, nipping at her lip in a sort of sensual punishment. "Don't you dare ever leave me like that again without telling me goodbye!"

She shivered, feeling as if she were flying high on sexual need. "Okay," she finally replied, not sure what else to say. Then his words hit her. The meaning behind the words meant...did he...?

"Um...does that mean that...you want...?" she couldn't finish that question, too embarrassed to ask and too afraid of the potential answers.

"Hell yes, I want another night with you. Not just one more night though." He eyed her carefully. "What do you want?"

Wasn't that the million dollar question? "I don't know."

He lifted a dark eyebrow, chuckling. "I've known you long enough to know that you do know, but you're not going to admit it until you understand what's going on." He paused, looking at her carefully. "Am I right?"

Sloane didn't want to admit anything to him. First of all, she didn't understand what was...okay, he might be right there.

He smiled. "You're trying to understand all off the possible issues to having a relationship with me, aren't you?"

Sloane sighed, bowing her head slightly. "Yes. But..."

He wrapped his strong arms around her. "I get it, Sloane. It's one of the reason's you've been such an asset to me over the years. You need to understand the pros and cons, work through everything, and figure out ways to overcome potential problems." He took her hands in his, allowing her to put a bit of space between them without breaking contact. "The problem with that way of approaching this kind of situation is that we're two human beings and we can't anticipate every problem."

"That's true, but shouldn't we approach a...romantic relationship cautiously?"

His lips quirked. "I suspect that we've been approaching this relationship for the past several years."

Sloane wanted to believe him, but her tender, wounded heart wouldn't allow her to. Not after her personal history and her knowledge of men. She'd experienced her mother's pain after she'd informed Rayne and then Pepper's sperm donors, watched her mother fall apart when they disappeared, never to be heard from again. Sloane had helped her gentle, heartbroken mother pull herself together, encouraging and helping in any way she could. It was one of the reasons Sloane had so easily stepped into the mother-role after their mother was killed. It felt natural, probably because she'd been doing it for so long already.

Which isn't to say that she hadn't panicked many times during that period right after their mother's funeral. Especially the first night after they'd been evicted from the apartment. And the next several nights. Okay, so she'd never really stopped panicking, Sloane realized.

"I'm not sure if..."

"One day at a time, Sloane," he coaxed softly, and stood up, giving her hands a final squeeze before releasing them. "Just relax, Sloane. We'll figure this out *together.*"

She liked the sound of that. But she also preferred to be in control. He knew this about her and laughed softly as he walked into his office. "You're going to try to plan anyway, aren't you?" he asked over his shoulder.

She didn't reply, and instead turned to watch him walk away because...well, because watching Josh Starke at any point, coming or going, was a delight for the senses! He was so tall and confident, his shoulders broad, his stomach flat...she remembered exploring that flat stomach last night and realized that it wasn't exactly flat. It was ridged and amazing and...!

"Stop staring at me or I'm going to come over there and we're going to start tonight's activities early."

Sloane jumped, then blushed when he turned to smirk at her over his shoulder with those too-knowing eyes. "I wasn't...!"

"You were. But that's okay. Because I've been doing it to you for years," he admitted with a wink, and walked into his office.

Huh? Had he just admitted that he watched her walk away? Surely she'd misunderstood him. But even dismissing that possibility didn't eliminate the smile that bloomed as she returned to her computer.

It took all of Josh's willpower to walk into his office and not coax Sloane out of the office and back to his place. He'd been so furious when he'd woken up to discover that she was gone. Not just gone from his bed, but from his penthouse. He'd imagined her in his home so many times over the years, and to wake up and want to have her there, to see her shy smile and, perhaps, make love to her again. Hell, he'd like to take the whole damn day off just to make love to her.

So when he'd discovered that she was gone, he'd been ready to punch someone. Luckily, the doorman to his building had been behind a counter, so when the poor man had wished him a good morning as Josh had walked out, he'd been too far away for violence.

But now that he'd talked to her, warned her that they weren't finished after just one night, Josh felt better, more centered. Ready to take on the world!

Was he in a good mood because of the amazing sex? Or was it because he was going to repeat everything all over again, with a few variations on the original theme, tonight and the following nights?

Josh frowned as he turned on his computer. Something about that statement wasn't right. What was it? While he scanned the stock prices from the previous night's transactions in Asia and Europe, seeing the trends and forming plans, another part of his brain went over that thought. He realized almost immediately what didn't feel right.

He didn't want just a few more nights with Sloane. He wanted...forever. They'd worked together for years and he'd felt only half alive when she left at the end of each day. But last night, when they'd been working at his place, Josh had realized how much he loved having Sloane in his home. Thinking back even further, he knew that they'd worked at his place many nights over the years for that exact same reason. He loved having Sloane in his house. In his life. Hell, he didn't want her for a few nights or even a few months. He wanted her for the rest of his life.

Jerking upright at that thought, he looked through the door of his office. Vaguely, he heard the rest of the office stirring to life, the other brokers settling into their desks. But his focus was on Sloane, on the beautiful, delicate profile and the elegant arch of her neck. She'd put all of those damn pins back in her hair, he thought. His kiss of a few moments ago had dislodged her carefully sleek hair but the prim Ms. Abbot was now firmly back in place.

Smiling, his body reacted to the memory of her coming apart in his arms. Her sighs when he touched her in certain places. A lot of places, actually! Sloane might look like the cool, sophisticated businesswoman, but when he touched her, there was nothing cool about her. She was hot and beautiful and sexy and...his body tightened and Josh struggled to banish those memories for the moment. He couldn't do anything right now, but later, once the workday was over, he would act.

For the first time in his adult life, he wanted to push work issues aside and just...hell, he wanted to haul Sloane out of this damn office draped over his shoulder and make love to her for the next several days. Weeks! He'd thought about her so many times over the past eight years, he had several thousand fantasies to work his way through.

As he watched, Sloane's phone rang and she efficiently picked it up, answering with her normal professional tone. But last night, she hadn't sounded professional. At all.

With a smile, he pulled his eyes away and focused on work.

Chapter 15

All day long, there was one issue after another to deal with, so she hadn't had time to become overly nervous about Josh's comment about tonight. But now, the staff were slowly wrapping up for the day. Darkness had descended and she knew with every fiber of her being that Josh was going to take her into his arms and...and do those things to her again.

And everything inside of her warned her to get out of the office and find a place to hide. She had reasons. Valid reasons! Josh wasn't the forever kind of man and she...okay, he'd used protection last night. But...there was that freakish fertility in her family! And Sloane knew now that she'd been in love with Josh for too long! She was going to be hurt when he moved on to someone else, she thought. She'd have to find a new job, a new place to live. She'd have to...!

"Sloane?" his deep voice interrupted her litany.

Slowly, she turned away from her computer, her worried eyes looking into his dark, confident green ones. No, they weren't confident, she thought. They were heated and hungry! At that moment, Sloane was positive that she could have said no and he would have respected that answer.

Instead, she reacted to the hunger. The need. She reacted because she felt the same aching, desperate need flare to life inside of her.

"Are you ready to go?"

Sloane looked down, trying to hide the need, wishing she could cover it up.

"Stop," he ordered.

The one word pulled her gaze up to meet his. "Stop what?"

"Stop trying to hide from me, Sloane," he ordered. Moving towards her, he took her hands and pulled her to her feet. "I need you, Sloane.

84

More than oxygen, I need you. And I'm not afraid to admit it. Can you be honest with me? I suspect that what you are feeling might embarrass you. Or you might feel that I don't want that level of intensity. But let me just clear that up right now. I want you. I've wanted you for years," he admitted. "I told you before that this isn't just a one night thing. I want more than just one night with you. I want..." he hesitated, seeing the panic in her eyes. "Well, let's just take it one day at a time, okay?"

Josh felt her trembling increase as he spoke. Not wanting to terrify her, he stopped, waiting. But when she continued to stare up at him with that hunger, the same hunger he was feeling, he couldn't hold back any longer. He needed to hold her, to feel her pressed against his body. She was so damn soft and felt amazing when she pressed her breasts against him, shifting ever so slightly. It was almost as if she wanted to feel him but didn't want him to know how badly she wanted it.

But he wasn't an idiot. He'd worked with her for too long, observed her for eight long, agonizing years. Sloane was a planner. This sexual tension had been present from the moment he'd interviewed her, on his part, but it was probably new to her.

So, he kissed her. Just a gentle brush of his lips against hers, but he loved the feel of her lips, her mouth trembling ever so slightly. If he'd only felt that trembling, he might have pulled back, given her some space. But he felt her hand against his chest, her fingers sliding up, as if she wanted to feel him through the fabric of his dress shirt.

And he wanted that too! He wanted it so badly his body ached!

"Come home with me, Sloane," he urged. He saw the worry in her eyes, but didn't understand it. There were times when he could read her like a book, but this wasn't one of them.

"Could we...go to my place?" she whispered, almost choking out the words.

"Anything you want, honey."

And with that, he took her hand, grabbing her purse and her tote bag. He didn't give her a chance to change her mind. If she'd feel more comfortable at her tiny cottage, then they'd spent the next several hours there. He thought about protection, but he knew that he had something in his wallet. He doubted that she'd thought of that, but he'd protect her. At this moment though, it was imperative that they get the hell out of the office because he wasn't sure how much longer he could hold off.

"Wait!" she yelped when they were halfway to the door.

"Forget it," he ordered, tugging at her hand. "You're not bringing any work home tonight."

She smiled and he groaned when her cheeks turned that sexy pink again.

"No, it isn't that. I just need to close down my computer."

"Forget your computer."

"Josh! I lock it down for security reasons! I can't just leave it unlocked."

He understood finally and released her hand. She had a point and he couldn't believe he'd forgotten about something so essential. Their client's financial data was on the system and leaving the computer unlocked would be a dangerous thing.

But so was her bending over her desk like that.

"I just need to finish this e-mail," she told him, typing furiously.

Josh stood there, his eyes moving over the roundness of her bottom in the skirt. He could just...lift that material up and reveal her demure panties. He'd discovered last night that she preferred the plain, simple cotton panties. He imagined taking her to a lingerie store and dressing her in lace and satin. Would she let him? She was so adorably frugal. He'd bet she bought her panties and bras at the discount stores, not wanting to spend money on anything as frivolous as sexy underwear. But she had a very fine ass and he wanted to see her in lace. Black lace. No, red! Yeah, she had beautiful, pale skin that would look amazing in red lace.

Damn, he was hard and throbbing already. Moving closer, he ran a finger down her spine, smiling when she stiffened. He understood that her natural inclination was to reject any sort of touch because touching wasn't professional. But...he moved his hand back down her back and... yes! Her body melted, her fingers moved off of the keyboard, gripping the wood of the desk. Her breathing changed, becoming ragged and he'd guess that her eyes were closed as she tried to fight the desire burning through her.

Just watching her, feeling her body melt against his hand just as it had last night, made his body throb harder.

Damn, he shouldn't have touched her, he realized. "We're not going to make it out of here," he warned a moment before he pulled her around and kissed her.

Her arms wrapped around his neck, silently telling him that she needed this just as intensely. That was the point of no return for Josh. He pulled at her clothes, almost pulling the buttons off her blouse. He didn't bother taking her skirt off, he simply pushed it higher. Vaguely, he realized that she was doing the same thing to his clothes, but he was too focused on getting to her, revealing her skin. He slid the silk blouse off her shoulders, revealing the creamy globes of her breasts and her already taut, pink nipples. He leaned her back so that she was laid out on her desk, her hips shifting against his erection now that he'd pressed his hips between her legs. She might still have her shoes on, but he didn't know. A small part of his brain wanted to look, wanting to see her sexy heels and revel at her long legs wrapped around his waist, but he couldn't split his focus. He needed to be inside of her, feeling her clench around his erection.

His mouth latched onto her nipple and he heard her cry out, felt her shiver as her fingers dove into his hair, silently begging for more.

He barely took the time to move over to her other breast before moving lower, needing a taste. Just a small taste he promised himself. A small taste, and then...!

"You're so wet!" he groaned, inhaling her musky, feminine scent. She was like a glistening, pink enticement!

"We can't do this here!" she gasped, suddenly realizing what was about to happen.

He only laughed harshly. "Oh yes we can!" he vowed. "Let me show you how." And with that, he lifted her legs over his shoulders, and pressed his hand against her stomach, holding her in place. He'd learned that he needed one hand on her stomach and another hand wrapped around her leg to hold her in place. Just the anticipation of feeling her climax against his mouth was making him lose control!

Sloane was so primed and ready for him that she jerked at the first touch of his mouth against that sensitive nub. Her fingers tightened in his hair, almost pressing against his head as if she wanted to guide him but was too shy to actually be so bold. Damn, he loved that! He couldn't wait until she was comfortable enough with him to actually show him, to use her hands to guide his mouth.

Hell, he couldn't think about that just yet or he'd lose it!

She tasted even better than he remembered. She was delicious and so damned responsive. Too soon, she was splintering apart, her screams echoing through the empty office. After one more lingering taste, he moved up her stomach, kissing and nibbling as the hand that had been holding her still around her leg moved to soothe her as she came down from her first climax.

He stood and fumbled with his wallet, letting it fall to the floor as soon as his fingers found the condom. It took him seconds to get the foil packet opened and the protection rolled down his shaft. When he looked up, he discovered Sloane watching him, her tongue darting out to wet her lips.

"Don't do that," he ordered, pulling her to the edge of the desk. With a slow, easy thrust, he pressed into her heat.

"Don't do what?" she gasped, trying to lift her hips, but because she was on the edge, she had no leverage. He was completely in control. Sloane could only whimper as he looked down at where their bodies were connected, watching those pink, glistening folds give way as he pressed into her.

It was a hypnotic sight! That, combined with those gasping sighs and delicious whimpers was eroding his control.

With one hand, he pressed his thumb against that nub, helping her along. In almost no time, he felt her tightening around his shaft and closed his eyes, fighting to hold back until...she screamed, her body throbbing as a second climax rolled over her. That was all he could take and he growled as he thrust faster and faster. Josh wanted this to last longer, but she felt so damn good and he was only able to enjoy a few more thrusts before her body pulled him into a mind-bending orgasm.

Sloane stared up at the ceiling, stunned at what had just happened. Had it been this good last night? "Wow!" she whispered, and bit her lip, shocked that she'd said it out loud.

Josh lifted his head and looked down at her, a playful smile making his eyes sparkle. Had she ever thought he was harsh looking? How could a man with eyes that beautiful be harsh?

"I agree," he said with a chuckle.

He pulled away and Sloane bit her lip. She'd like to stay just like this for a bit longer. His head nestled against her neck, his body still intimately connected with hers, and it felt so good to be in his arms like this.

She moaned wistfully as he pulled out of her. But since she was basically naked, spread out on her desk in a completely undignified manner, she hurried to pull herself together. It took a bit of work to get her fingers to work the buttons back into place. In the end, it was Josh who finished the process, his knuckles brushing against her breasts in the most delicious way.

"Are you doing that on purpose?' she asked, suspicion lacing her voice.

"Yeah," he laughed. He grabbed his jacket, which had fallen to the floor at some point, and buckled his belt.

"Good grief!" she gasped, jumping off of the desk and looking around. The door to her office was closed, but the door leading into his private office was still open. Anyone still in the building could have walked into Josh's office and seen them...on her desk!

Josh must have read her horrified expression, because he put a finger under her chin, lifting her face so that she was looking into his eyes.

"No one is here, honey," he promised. "And I lock my door every night. Security," he teased, reminding her that security was the issue that had slowed their departure in the first place.

Sloane couldn't help it, she laughed, feeling free and relaxed for the first time today. The laughter resounded through the empty offices as she entered the code on her computer, glancing over her shoulder at Josh. Sure enough, he was staring at her bottom again.

"No!" she told him, but the sparkle in her eyes showed she wasn't completely serious.

And of course, Josh was terrible at taking orders so as soon as she turned around to finish with her password, he reached for her bottom again. Sloane swung around, squeaking with outrage. But he only moved his hands to her waist, pulling her against him. "Damn, I want to hear that sound again, but when I have my mouth on you."

She pulled back, shocked at his lack of inhibitions and also oddly fascinated by the intensity in his eyes, silently telling her that he wasn't kidding.

"Let's get out of here. If you keep looking at me like that, we're going to make use of the sofa in my office and I want a bed the next time I'm inside of you."

He didn't give her a chance to argue. He took her hand again, grabbed her purse and tote bag, and headed for the door. She trailed after him, smothering a laugh at his urgency. In truth, she was flattered that he wanted her with this kind of intensity. She'd dated in the past, but no man had ever made her feel this beautiful and wanted. Of course, she'd never wanted any man the way she wanted Josh. No man had ever measured up to Josh. None had the same kind of brilliance and intensity or the charisma the man emanated.

So, Sloane didn't hesitate as he rushed her out. At least, not until they reached the outer door and she realized that something was missing. She froze, pulling against his hand that was still holding hers.

"What's wrong?" he demanded, turning and coming back to her.

"Um...I'm missing something," she whispered, looking around warily to make sure that no one could hear her.

Josh's eyes laughed. "What would you be missing?" he asked, moving closer, his hands shifting on her waist to pull her against his body.

"My underwear!" she replied back in a horrified whisper.

He threw back his head, laughing and hugged her.

"Never change, Sloane," he asked. "Please, never change! I love making you blush."

She squirmed against him.

"I think they are on the floor in my office. I'll just run back and...!"

"They are in my pocket and I'm sorry, my dear, but they are torn and wouldn't do you much good." He lowered his head, nibbling along her neck. "I was a bit too vehement in my efforts before." He lifted his mouth from her neck and she tried hard not to whimper at the loss of that touch. But his nose lightly brushed against the shell of her ear as he whispered, "I'll replace them, but not tonight."

With that, he led her out of the office and into the parking lot, leading her over to his Mercedes sedan. "We're going to your place and I'm not letting you out of bed until morning."

Sloane grinned up at him as she pulled her legs inside before he closed the door. As she watched him walk around to the driver's side, she smiled, thinking that life was pretty darn good right now!

Chapter 16

How had her life gone so off track?

Sloane stared at the calendar and rechecked the date. Surely she wasn't...! Impossible!

Flipping back to the previous month, sure enough, the notation on the sixteenth of the previous month was right there. She flipped to the previous month, hoping that it wasn't on the expected date. But yep. There was the notation on the eighteenth. Twenty-eight days prior.

Sloane was about as regular with her periods as was humanly possible. From about the age of sixteen until now, her periods had always been twenty-eight days apart. Like clockwork. So that could only mean ....!

Swallowing, she flipped back to the month before. Then the month before that. Twenty-eight days. Going back to the current month, she went through every day, looking for the notation, praying that she'd put it somewhere. Or that maybe this month, she'd simply forgotten to type in the notation.

Nothing. She reviewed the meetings during the month, trying to remember if she'd had her period during the previous two weeks. But nope. There wasn't anything that might remind her that she'd had her period.

She was two weeks late! Not two days, which she could dismiss, even though she was so regular, it was irritating. Two whole weeks.

Rubbing her forehead, she stared blankly at the calendar, hating herself because she knew better! She'd preached safe sex and dual contraception to Rayne and Pepper so many times over the years, they groaned whenever she brought up the subject.

And yet, she hadn't followed her own rule. Oh, she'd gone to the doctor's office and she had a prescription for birth control! Yep, she'd done the right thing. But she'd gone after she and Josh had become sexually active. According to the calendar, it wouldn't have made a difference anyway. She'd most likely gotten pregnant that first night with him.

He was a powerful man. And the women in her family had freakish levels of fertility! She knew this. She'd preached this fact! She'd lived with the consequences of that issue all her life, not having a father around. So, why was she now surprised that using a condom, using just one method of birth control, hadn't been sufficient?

Sloane glanced at the closed door between her office and Josh's. Should she tell him?

Sloane's arms wrapped around her stomach and her thoughts flashed back to the nights she'd heard her mother crying. Those nights always preceded the announcement that she was pregnant and Sloane was going to have a sibling. It also warned Sloane that the man her mother had been dating would no longer be coming around.

And it meant that the finances would be painfully tight. Her mother had been a hair stylist and, although she was very good with a pair of scissors, she had to work almost every day in order to get paid. Having a baby meant that her mother had to take time off, which meant no tips, no payment from her regular clients, and a lot of stress while her mother recovered from giving birth.

Sloane had adored both of her sisters from the moment her mother had come home from the hospital. Rayne had been a pale little lump with big, blue eyes and a red tuft of hair on the top of her head, although Sloane had been very young at that point. Pepper had been an adorable baby, exuberant from the first moment she'd come home. Sloane had been old enough to help diaper Pepper, feed her, and hold her at night...well, hold the tiny bundle when her mother placed Pepper carefully in Sloane's arms.

And now, she suspected that she was pregnant. In the same situation as her mother! Rubbing her forehead, she wondered what she was going to do.

"Money," she whispered and looked over her shoulder to make sure that no one was about to come into her office. When she was assured that she was still alone, she clicked on the keys, logging into her bank account. She saw the balance there and sighed with relief. Right after that, she logged into her retirement and investment accounts, both of which Josh had convinced her to open once she understood how good he was at making money grow. Both of her accounts were very healthy, thanks to Josh's brilliance.

"Checking your balances?" his deep voice teased.

Sloane swung around, startled that he had snuck up on her. "Oh, um...! Yes. I just...I log in every once in a while just to see the progress."

"I log in more often. Your account, along with your sisters' accounts, are a top priority for me."

Sloane's mouth fell open, but why should she be surprised? Josh had always been a very generous employer, but she hadn't been aware that he took a personal interest in her investment accounts. "You do?"

"Of course," he replied, straightening and tossing some papers onto her desk. "Can you make sure that these are taken care of?"

She blinked, realizing that this was another example of how Josh didn't want anyone to know what a good guy he was. Despite her fear that she was pregnant, Sloane couldn't hide her smile. He tried so hard to be such a grump, but she'd learned that his grumpy attitude was a defense mechanism. His way of hiding what a wonderful man he actually was. He didn't like anyone knowing about the good things he'd done. Nor did he like people thanking him for his generosity.

"Yes, of course," she replied and took the papers, her eyes skimming over the words but not absorbing the information.

Surely, she wasn't, Sloane told herself. She couldn't be! Sloane was the responsible sister. She was the oldest, the role model! She couldn't be pregnant!

Josh left for his next meeting as another thought occurred to her. She swiveled around, her fingers flying over the keyboard as she pulled up the company's maternity leave policy. She'd never had reason to explore this issue, but with relief, she discovered that Josh's company was very generous, allowing each employee a full three months of paid leave. Most American companies didn't pay the employee while they were out on maternity leave, although almost all companies were required to bring the woman back after she gave birth.

But could she stay employed here? Would Josh let her stay on? She doubted it. He'd probably ask her to leave. Being pregnant with his child, he'd be too embarrassed to keep her as his assistant.

"I'm a cliché," she whispered miserably.

"What's that?" he asked, his eyes narrowing as he stepped back into her office.

"Nothing!" she replied, straightening her shoulders. Her first priority would be to confirm the pregnancy. A test, she thought as he eyed her curiously. She'd have to stop by a drugstore after work and get a test.

But Josh came home with her or he drove her to his place every night! They'd been together every night for the past month!

Josh walked back into Sloane's office, taking in the tension in her shoulders and caught her rubbing her forehead. Something was wrong.

He'd sensed it earlier, but now he was sure.

"What's going on?' he demanded, itching to fix anything that was causing her stress.

Even as he watched, he saw her shoulders tighten further. But she forced her lips into a smile. "Nothing!"

She was lying and he wondered why. Sloane was one of the most honest people he'd ever met. Others could lie and he'd expect it, anticipate it even. But Sloane? She was brutally honest.

So, what was wrong? Why was she lying now?

"Sloane, we need to talk," he began. Her eyes turned frantic. Shaking her head, she leapt to her feet, keeping her eyes on her desk. "I need to go do...something," she told him. "I'm sorry, but would you mind if we...?"

"You need time alone?" he offered, even though he hated the idea. They'd been together every damn night since that first time. And at no point had she even hinted at the need for time alone! No, this was different. She was upset and it infuriated him that she was turning away from him when she was upset. Didn't she know that he would help her? That she could rely on him for more than just sex?

She shook her head, then nodded reluctantly. "I'm sorry, I have a personal errand to run. I'll..." she looked around nervously. "I'll make up the time, but I have to...I need to go do...something." And then she was gone!

Damn it! Josh couldn't remember the last time he'd been so angry! And hurt? Hell, he didn't like to think of himself as being someone who could be hurt, but...yeah, he was hurt that she'd turned away from him when she was upset.

Furthermore, she'd been perfectly fine this morning. He'd made sure that she'd been more than fine this morning before they'd separated to get ready for work. He was absolutely positive that she'd climaxed in his arms this morning. Twice!

Yes, she'd left his place with a smile this morning, heading back to her cottage to shower and change clothes.

That was another thing, he thought. There was absolutely no reason why she needed to go back to her place every morning. She should just move into his place! He'd teased her about it several times over the past several weeks, wanting her to be with him more than for just the nights.

Whatever had upset her today only proved that he wanted her with him. Damn it, she'd proven over and over again that she could handle life on her own. She was strong and capable, able to handle everything life and work tossed at her. So, there was no reason for her to keep trying to prove herself.

And damn it, he wanted to take care of her! Josh wanted to shower her with luxuries and pamper her. He wanted to take her shopping and dress her in designer clothes. Then take her back to his place and strip off all of her clothes and make love to her until she was gasping for breath.

Unfortunately, every time he'd brought up the idea of her just bringing a bag with extra clothes to his place, she'd resisted. Sloane kept saying that bringing clothes would mean something that "they weren't doing", whatever the hell that meant.

What weren't they doing? She came over to his place after work every damn day! He'd cook dinner, they'd eat, then clean up dinner together. After dinner, they'd sit and talk, finish work issues, or just sit and read together. And they'd make love together every damn night! She slept in his arms, damn it! She curled up against him! His shoulder was her pillow and she slept contentedly...until she shifted against him during the night or in the morning. At which point, he'd make love to her all over again.

Damn, was he hurting her? Was she not interested in sex that often? But he wasn't always the one that initiated their sexual encounters. Yeah, at first, he'd been the one that initiated. Lately though, she'd become bolder and he loved it!

Running a hand through his hair, he wondered if someone had said or done something. Was the work too much for her? Had someone asked her to do something that she hadn't...?

No. From the very first day she'd come on board with Josh, she'd been a powerhouse, accomplishing every task he'd thrown at her! Sloane never shied away from a challenge. Hell, she thrived on challenges! He remembered a few days over the years when she'd gotten everything done and she'd wandered into his office, asking if he needed help with anything.

He'd silently laughed at her, thinking she was beautiful. And sexy. And...amazing! Yeah, he'd been in love with her almost from that first day.

So, what the hell was wrong today? And why hadn't she come to him with whatever it was?

Glancing over at the papers and files on her desk, he moved closer. Her desk was a mess! That amplified his concern. Sloane was obsessively organized. She never allowed anything to be out of place and she never, ever, left her office without storing all documents away in the filing cabinet and ensuring that all information was securely locked down. There was too much danger in leaving someone's financial information out for her to slack off.

Damn it, even her computer was unlocked!

He moved over and sat down in her chair, shifting the mouse so that he could lock things down before heading out to find her. But something caught his eye. Why was she looking up events from previous months? Carefully, he clicked on each meeting notation, but every one of them were his meeting dates and times. He'd been in these meetings, and he didn't remember any issue with....

Josh clicked on another meeting, one he didn't recognize. Everything else on the calendar was familiar but this one...

He looked back at the previous month and, sure enough, the same exact meeting was there, but not on the same day. He clicked on the various meetings around that one, recognizing all of them, but not that one. Again, he flipped to the previous month and...sure enough, that exact same meeting was there.

Leaning back in his chair, his eyes narrowed on the meeting notation. "TOM in town." Tom? Who the hell was Tom? He flipped through the company's client list and came up with several clients named Tom or Thomas, but as far as he knew, these clients hadn't ever come for a visit. Most of their clients were advised over the phone or via computer. Because his business was far flung, it wasn't possible for his team of investors to meet with each of their clients face to face on a regular basis.

So, who the hell was Tom?

A burning acidic anger streaked through his stomach at the thought of this Tom person touching Sloane! Clicking through, he realized that he came to town every damn month! Who was he? And why did he only visit Sloane once a month?

Wait.

Once a month.

The term echoed through his thoughts.

Josh clicked again. Tom hadn't visited recently. Not since the first night that he'd been with Sloane.

That made him feel better briefly, but that phrase kept swirling through his mind.

Once a month.

When it came to him, Josh leapt to his feet, then he almost fell to the floor. She had someone...or something...visit once a month? He slumped back down in Sloane's chair, his mind reeling. But not this month!

Once a month. No! Pregnant? Was Sloane pregnant?

But...he always used protection! And Sloane had mentioned something about getting on birth control. His stomach tightened. But one thought glowed. A baby!

Damn, Sloane would look so beautiful pregnant! And she'd be the most amazing mother!

A baby! Could she be pregnant? They'd both been so careful, but condoms weren't one hundred percent effective. And some of their nights together had been pretty...impatient. In fact, most of their times together, at least the first time each night, was a bit frantic. Okay, maybe a more than "a bit" frantic.

Josh rubbed the back of his neck. If she was pregnant, was she feeling okay? Was she sick? He knew that most women suffered from morning sickness during pregnancy and he didn't like the idea of her being sick. Not even if it was natural and normal. Just the thought of her dealing with morning sickness made him feel nauseous and uncomfortable.

A baby!

Was she scared? He remembered her telling him about her father. Wait, how had she referred to the man? "A sperm donor", because he'd gotten Sloane's mother pregnant, then vanished, never to be heard of again.

How could he have done that? He'd just created a life! Josh wanted to hunt the man down and do him bodily harm. Kids needed fathers and, if Sloane were pregnant, then he damn well was going to be there for their child! Every day, he'd be there! And he'd be there for Sloane as well. She'd never have to worry about money. Never! Okay, so he knew that she was pretty well set financially already. He'd invested her money in the best stocks and funds and ensured that she and her sisters would never have to worry about money. But he wanted more for his child. He wanted more for Sloane! He wanted...!

Josh thought back to his initial hope, that she'd let him pamper her.

His child was going to be spoiled, he thought with a tiny smile. But not too spoiled! No, he couldn't let their children become spoiled brats. They were a bane to society. His children, their kids, would be responsible! Not spoiled.

Josh closed his eyes, trying to figure out how to give his children every advantage and yet, not raise spoiled children. It was a mystery that he wasn't fully prepared to figure out just yet.

"I need to find out if she's actually pregnant," he muttered out loud.

Standing up, he headed for his office, intending to grab his car keys and go find Sloane, demand to know if she was pregnant. Then he froze. "Security," he grumbled, turning around and moving back to the desk. He locked down her computer, and gathered the files from her desk, bringing them back to his office where he locked them away in his desk. With everything secure, he grabbed his keys.

"Time to get some answers," he muttered.

Chapter 17

Sloane stared at the box, reading the directions for the tenth time. "Seriously? I pee on a stick and...and that's it?" She sighed, pacing the small confines of the den. She'd gone to the drug store right after leaving the office.

With a groan, she closed her eyes and leaned her head back. "Just take the test," she said out loud.

And still she paced, clenching the box as if letting it go might cause it to bite her.

Turning, she saw movement out of the corner of her eye. Thinking it was Wilma and she could ask her friend for advice, she hurried to the door, pulling it open. Wilma sometimes stopped by when Sloane came home from work, often dropping off dinner or a dessert. Over the years, Wilma had sort of become a mother-like figure for Sloane and her sisters, she had never invaded their privacy and yet, she was always there to offer a hug or sage advice.

But this wasn't Wilma rounding the corner. It was Josh! His powerful, black Mercedes pulled to a stop right next to her sensible, much less expensive sedan.

"Shoot!" she hissed, wishing that she'd hidden her car. But even as she thought it, Sloane discarded the option. "Not like I could hide it from him. It's a car and there isn't really a lot of hiding places around for something that big."

He stepped out of his car and looked at her. Instantly, Sloane knew that he knew! How could he know? Those green eyes narrowed and she tried valiantly to banish the stress she knew showed on her face. Well, not banish it exactly. But hide it. Josh wouldn't want to know if she was pregnant, she thought as she watched him walk towards her.

Goodness, he was so strong and vital. The man didn't really walk so much as prowl, she noticed, not for the first time. She remembered meeting him that first day and she'd thought him dangerous then. Now she knew that he was a sweet, gentle, kind man. Merciless in business, but he'd never hurt her.

Of course, he didn't know that she was pregnant. Or might be, she thought. Looking down, she realized that she was still holding pregnancy test. She hid her hand behind her back, then looked up at Josh.

His eyes narrowed suspiciously as he neared the doorway.

"Are you okay?" he asked, his voice deep and husky. Usually, she only heard that tone when he was making love to her.

He stopped less than a foot from her, hands fisted on his hips and a concerned look in his wonderful, green eyes. "Yes. I'm fine," she lied. For the second time in her life, she'd lied to Josh and it felt so completely wrong.

He didn't stop when he moved closer and her heart pounded in her chest. He smelled so good and she knew from the past several weeks that he felt even better. When he pulled her into his arms...yeah, just like that!

"You're not okay," he replied gruffly.

Sloane wasn't strong enough to resist the warmth and security of Josh's arms. Instead of pulling away as she knew that she should, Sloane leaned into him, resting her head against his hard chest, breathing in the scent of man and spicy aftershave. He smelled so wonderful, she thought, closing her eyes against sudden tears. A sob broke through her control. Then another. And another until she couldn't stop the tears or the inelegant sobs. She wasn't aware of Josh lifting her into his arms, but she felt him cradle her and she pressed her face against the warmth of his neck, letting go of the tension that had been building inside of her. Her body shook with sobs and his arms tightened around her, just holding her until the storm passed.

When she took another deep, shaky breath, then pulled away, he looked down into her eyes, wiping away some of the tears with a thumb. "Feel better?" he asked gently.

Sloane nodded, lifting dewy eyes up to his. "I'm sorry. I don't know where all of that came from."

"You're worried about being pregnant," he replied calmly.

Stiffening, she looked up at him.

She started to slide off of his lap, her breath catching in her throat. He'd leave her if she admitted it! Sloane couldn't take that right now and she realized that, in the back of her mind, she'd decided that even if she was pregnant, she wouldn't tell Josh. Not right away. She wanted more time with him, more time to deal with the heartache of him walking away.

"No! I'm not!" she lied again, and cringed. She really hated lying to him like this. It was so wrong! "At least, I don't *know* if I am or not."

He pulled the forgotten box out of her hands. "Why don't you go take this pregnancy test and find out?" he suggested, those green eyes filled with gentle firmness. "Then we'll figure out what to do next, no matter what the test says."

Sloane didn't move. She simply sat there on his lap, staring at the box.

"No matter what," he vowed again. "I'm not going to disappear. Not even if you're pregnant, Sloane. I love you. I'm not going anywhere. In fact," he paused and shifted her slightly, reaching behind her and bringing forward a small, black box, opening the lid. "No matter what, I want to marry you, Sloane Abbot. I want to spend the rest of my life with you."

She stared, stunned at the beautiful diamond ring nestled in the black velvet interior. It was a gorgeous square, center diamond with smaller diamonds lining the edge, then more diamonds along the top of the setting. She couldn't even guess as to its worth, but it was the most beautiful ring she'd ever seen!

"You...you want to marry me?" she whispered.

"Yes. I don't care if you're pregnant or not." He paused, and shook his head. "No, let me correct that. I'd *love* it if you were pregnant. I want to have kids, Sloane. I want a family. But only with you. I've dreamed about you for so damn long, and you're finally in my arms every night. I want to make it official. I want you to move in with me. Today. Immediately. I don't want to hide my feelings anymore for fear that I might scare you away. Seeing you worried this afternoon shook me, reminded me that I had no official claim on you." He took her hand, squeezing her fingers. "I want that, Sloane. I want to be the man that you turn to when you're upset. I want to be the man that helps you through the hard times, the one that you come to when you're excited or happy about something." He leaned forward, taking the ring out of the box and sliding it onto her finger. "I want you, Sloane. All of you. Will you marry me? Before you take that pregnancy test, answer that for me. Because I want no misunderstanding about this. I want to marry you because I'm in love with you. Not because you may be pregnant."

Sloane swallowed hard after that beautiful speech, not sure what to say. She wasn't even sure if she could speak! Never in her life had she ever imagined anyone saying something like that to her. He wanted her because...he loved her?

"I think I'd given up on someone loving me," she replied, staring at the diamond on her finger.

"Because you think your father didn't love you?"

She shrugged, not wanting to admit that one person had so much influence in her life. "Maybe," she hedged. Then she looked up at him. "Or maybe it's because I've been in love with you for so many years that..."

The rest of her sentence was lost because Josh kissed her, his arms tightening around her until she could barely breathe. When he finally lifted his mouth, she was stunned by the passion in his eyes.

"Say it again," he urged.

"I love you," she whispered, wondering if she'd ever be able to say those words without feeling this quivering terror in her chest.

"I love you too," he told her, and bent his head, kissing her again but more gently this time. Over and over, he brushed his lips against hers until she couldn't take the teasing any longer. She lifted her hands, bringing his head down to hers and kissed him with all of the love in her heart.

He laughed, pulling her hands away. "If we don't stop that, then you're never going to give me the answer I want to hear."

"I love you," she whispered again, her fingers and eyes tracing over his facial features, stunned by the luck in her life.

He chuckled, and kissed her again. "That's nice to hear, but not what I'm waiting for."

"Marriage?" she whispered.

"Yes. Marriage. I want all of you. And I want to know that you can accept all of me, quirks, temperament, and all."

She laughed, delighted. "I've dealt with you for the last eight years," she replied.

He grinned slightly. "Think you could handle me for the next eighty years?"

Sloane threw her arms around his neck. "Yes!" she gasped, shocked that this was happening to her. The dream! It was the most beautiful dream coming to life!

He laughed, pulling her closer. "Damn, I never thought you'd finally agree!"

She laughed as well, relief surging through her in a wave that was so powerful, she felt a bit dizzy. Then he kissed her again and she let her fingers slide underneath his jacket, feeling his powerful muscles bunch and tense under her touch. But she didn't stop, needing to feel him, needing this proof that he wanted her.

A long time later, they were both breathing heavily in her bed, the sheets and pillows...somewhere. Josh groaned, pulling her against him and she smiled contentedly as she snuggled into his side.

"So, you're going to move in with me tonight, right?" he asked.

She smiled, feeling a glow of happiness warm her body. Or maybe it was the heat of his body that was warming her. The man had muscles packed onto muscles, which made him feel like a furnace heating the front of her body while his hands skimmed up and down her back.

"Move in with you?"

She thought about that for a moment, then the flash of light caught her eyes and she turned her hand, staring at the ring. The ring that meant that he truly loved her. That this wasn't just a dream where she'd wake up the following morning and feel that painful stab of sadness and loneliness that had gripped her world so many times over the years since she'd met him.

This was real.

She turned her head. "Do you *really* want to marry me?"

He looked at her, blue eyes clashing with green. Slowly, he nodded. "Yeah. I've been in love with you for so long, Sloane. I won't settle for anything less than marriage," he vowed. And with that, he kissed her. This wasn't a kiss of passion. It was a promise. A kiss for the future. Together.

Epilogue

"What's wrong?" Josh demanded, standing at her desk and glaring down at her, but the ferocious look wasn't as effective when he put a hand on his own flat, taut stomach.

"More nausea?" she asked, pulling open her drawer and taking out a box of gingersnaps, which she handed to him.

"Cookies?"

She smothered her amusement. So far, she'd had an absolutely wonderful pregnancy. No morning sickness, no pains, no problems at all. Josh, on the other hand, hadn't been so lucky. The nurses and doctors at the obstetrician's office laughed every time they came in. They'd heard of the father having sympathy pains before, but Josh took that to a whole new level. He never threw up, but he'd had a constant upset stomach since she'd finally taken the pregnancy test, which had confirmed that she was truly pregnant. He'd also had headaches, back pain, mood swings, and had been grouchy a lot lately.

"Yes. Ginger is supposed to ease the nausea. See if that works."

He rolled his eyes and set the box down on her desk, refusing to give in. He'd already been to his doctor who had done numerous tests, then declared him to be one of the healthiest patients he'd ever seen and diagnosed him with pregnancy sympathy pain.

"I'm fine," he replied with disdain. "You're changing the subject."

She stood up and pulled a chair closer to her desk, putting a hand on his shoulder to force him to sit down. "I'm not the one that fell asleep at seven o'clock last night, dear," she replied, kissing his cheek to sooth his wounded male pride.

"How much longer on this pregnancy?" he growled, rubbing his forehead.

She couldn't stop the giggle when he rubbed a hand over his chest, then looked at his hand.

"Stop looking at me!" he grumbled.

Sloane looked down at his groin. Sure enough, he was fully erect. "I love being pregnant!" she whispered.

He grabbed her hand. "I never knew that a woman in her fifth month of pregnancy could be so voracious!"

She smiled, a seductive look that she knew drove him wild. "That's one part of this pregnancy you can't complain about."

He chuckled. "I love that aspect. It's the fact that I fell asleep at seven o'clock last night that I don't like!"

She laughed again, leaning back slightly. "I'll admit, having you take over all of my pregnancy discomfort is truly amazing!"

He growled, taking her hand and pulling her forward. "Yeah, but payback is hell!"

She rolled her eyes. "Why are you threatening payback?"

"Because I'm the one getting tired, having the morning sickness, and dealing with the back problems!" he snapped. "This is embarrassing!"

She laughed, delighted with his grumpiness. "I think it's only fair. I'm the one carrying the baby."

"Yeah, but you look sexy as hell. While I just keep getting all of the negative stuff."

Sloane shrugged, but she felt...amazingly alive! Partly because of the pregnancy, and partly because she loved him so much.

"You changed the subject," he realized. "What's worrying you?"

Sloane's amusement disappeared. "Rayne isn't coming home for the holidays," she explained. "Apparently, she has some big project she's working on. I even told her that we could fly out to see her instead."

"What did she say to that?" he asked. "I can have my pilot fly to New York to get Pepper and we could be in San Diego by morning."

She lifted a hand, touching his cheek as she smiled to him. "You're so sweet to offer. But I already offered to fly out there for the holidays. She told me not to. She said that she really had to push hard to make her deadlines and that we'd just be in the way."

Josh's eyebrows went lower over those green eyes of his. "That doesn't sound like Rayne," he replied.

"I know!" She sighed, rubbing her forehead. "Something is wrong, Josh. I just...I can't figure out what's going on. We talk via Skype all the time, so I know that she's healthy. And she seems happy, but...?"

"But what?"

Sloane shrugged. "Sometimes, her happiness seems a bit forced. Like she's actually sad but pretending to be happy."

"Let's just take a trip out there ourselves and find out what's going on."

Sloane bit her lip. "Do you think that's a good idea?"

"Why not?" he challenged. "I've wanted to head out to San Diego to check on a few investment opportunities anyway but held off, wanting to be here with you."

Sloane blinked, her hand moving to cover her stomach. "Wait a minute. Have you been holding back because I'm pregnant?"

"Yes," he replied evenly. "And I'm not going to apologize for it either," he told her firmly. "You're my first priority, Sloane," he told her firmly. "You and this baby are too important to me. I'm not going to allow any unnecessary stress."

She thought he was the sweetest man alive! "But you're willing to fly out to San Diego now?"

His fingers squeezed hers with silent support. "Something is wrong with your sister. That means that you're worrying." He took her hand and pulled her onto his lap, hugging her close despite her rounded belly and extra weight. "If you're worrying, then so is the baby," he explained, putting a hand over her stomach. "So we'll fly out to San Diego. We'll review these businesses and, while we're there, we'll take Rayne out to dinner and you can see for yourself that she's okay."

He kissed the top of her head. "I don't want you worrying, Sloane. It isn't good for the baby and you don't sleep well."

She grinned and snuggled closer, loving the way he was so affectionate now. "Fine. As long as you have other business in the area. I don't want you to fly out there just for me."

"Rayne is my sister-in-law now," he told her, lifting her hand to kiss the gold band nestled against the edge of her diamond ring. "I'm concerned as well. She's family."

Sloane smiled, leaning against him more completely. "Thank you," she whispered. "Have I mentioned that I love you?"

He kissed her softly. "I'll never get tired of hearing it," he replied. "I love you too."

"And thank you for taking such good care of me and my family." Her hand brushed against his chest, her fingers teasing his flat male nipple.

Immediately, she was scooped into his arms and carried down the hallway to his bedroom. "You're doing that on purpose!" he growled before setting her down beside the bed and stripping off her clothes.

Sloane laughed, delighted with his urgency, but her fingers were just as frantic to get his clothes off. In the end, they didn't get naked, her fingers brushed his nipples too often so he simply twisted around so that she was straddling his hips while he lay back on the bed and, protecting her belly, thrust into her again and again, his fingers finding all of those delicious places on her body that drove her wild. Buried deep inside of her like this, he felt every tremble of her tight, wet body. His fingers teased her nipples while he thrust harder and faster, eventually moving down her body to grasp her hips with one hand while his other teased that nub, gently, then faster and harder until he heard her cry out with her release. Only then would he let his own body tumble over to a climax that just seemed more intense and powerful with every encounter with this beautiful woman!

When she collapsed on top of him, Josh shifted, protecting her and the baby, but refusing to lose his connection with her.

"Damn, I love you, woman!" he sighed, wrapping his arm around her.

She smiled. "Marriage with you will never be dull," she laughed. "I love you too, Josh."

Kular had other intentions. Taking the key out of her hands, he pulled her around and pressed her back against the wall. "Have dinner with me tomorrow," he commanded.

Rayne looked up at him, her body tingling with...fear? Yes, she was terrified of what this man made her feel. But it was more than just fear. That sensation was mixed with equal parts anticipation. He was going to kiss her. Rayne knew it with every fiber of her body!

"I can't."

"Can't?" he asked softly, his eyes moving over her features as if trying to memorize them. "Or won't?"

She wanted to laugh, feeling a bit light headed. "Can't. I have plans."

He didn't believe her, but for the life of her, she couldn't remember what Josh had planned for the next night. If Kular would just...step back, then maybe she would be able to think. Logic, her personal mantra, had disappeared when he'd stepped into her space.

"I'm going to kiss you, Rayne," he warned.

She stiffened and started to shake her head. Kiss her? She could barely control herself while he was just pressed against her! No way could she remain impassive if he kissed her!

But before she could speak, his mouth covered hers. For perhaps one second, maybe half a second, she resisted. After that moment, she was gone. His lips moved over hers with persuasive force and she shivered, her hands creeping slowly up to wind around his neck as his hands tugged at her hair, pulling her head back so that he could deepen the kiss. Over and over, his lips caressed hers until his tongue slid across her lips and she gasped. That's when his tongue slid into her mouth, deepening the kiss even more.

When he lifted his head, she stared up at him, willing him to kiss her again.

"I can't, love," he replied to her unspoken question. "Not unless you're willing to come back to my suite so that I can kiss you more thoroughly." He kissed her briefly, but pulled back. "And if that happens, then you should be prepared for marriage because I have no intention of letting you go."

She wasn't sure what he meant by that, but was warmed by the soft kiss of his lips against her forehead. He took the key from her hands and swiped it across the black square that released the door's lock. The click of the lock releasing was her only indication that she should move. But it still took a gentle shove from him before she entered the suite.

With only a backwards glance, she closed the door. Not because she wanted to, but because it seemed like the safest thing to do under the circumstances.

With a sigh, she leaned back against the door, closing her eyes against the sensual tingling that swamped her with desire.

Printed in Poland
by Amazon Fulfillment
Poland Sp. z o.o., Wrocław